Missionary Max and the Jungle Princess

Copyright © 2016 Andrew Comings

ISBN-10: 1503149560

ISBN-13: 978-1503149564

Illustrator | Zilson Costa

Publishing and Design Services | MelindaMartin.me

DEDICATION

This book is dedicated to my lovely wife, Itacyara, of whom the beautiful Ilana is but a poor reflection.

ACKNOWLEDGMENTS

Special thanks are in order for this second iteration of the Missionary Max saga:

To my Dad, Harold H. Comings, a writer in his own right, for giving me a love of stories and writing.

To my Mom, Judy C. Comings, who to this day corrects my grammar.

To Bob "the Killer" Miller, for introducing me to comic books way back then, and for providing essential feedback in the present.

To Bonnie Forrest, who did not laugh when I said I was thinking about being a writer.

To Tim, Vicki, Jason, Dan and Jeff Reiner, Jim and Julie Leonard, and all my other friends and colleagues in Brazil, who introduced me to the very real adventure of missionary life.

To Radyfran França, Daniel Simões, Genaldo Andrade, Fred Araujo, and all the other guys from the SBC dorm who, in one way or another, helped me to get rid of some of my "Americanisms" and taught me to love the Brazilian people.

To the city of São Luís, inspiration for Santo Expedito.

To Trey Schorr, for taking a risk on the first edition of this book.

To Zilson Costa, Brazilian comic book artist extraordinaire, who has brought Max and Ilana to life on the cover.

To Pete, Connie, Mom, everybody else who edited and otherwise gave feedback during the stages of development of this book.

Finally, and most important, to Jesus Christ, without whom this would be pointless.

PROLOGUE

"Yaaaaaaaaaaaaaaaaaaaaaaaaaaaaarrrrrrrrrrrgh!" The muscles of Maxwell Sherman's arms burned white-hot with exertion.

His hands clung desperately to a rope, while below him - several hundred feet below him - the jungle canopy spread out like a massive green carpet. In the distance he could make out the hazy blue of the Atlantic Ocean. From above came the sound of propellers.

He fought hard to pull himself up into the cockpit of the biplane from which the rope hung. It would have been a daunting task under any circumstances, and the beautiful woman in a leopard-skin dress with her arms and legs locked around his middle only made matters all the more difficult.

Gritting his teeth and gathering every last ounce of strength he possessed, Max began to climb.

Who is Max? Why are he and his lovely companion swinging like human pendulums over the jungle? To answer these questions, we must go back.

Way back.

The year was 1986, but on the island of Cabrito, it might as well have been 1956. Little had changed in three decades for inhabitants of this green speck in the middle of the Atlantic. The newest buildings in downtown Santo Expedito, Cabrito's sleepy capital city, had been built in the Seventies, but most of the structures that lined the cobblestone streets were from earlier decades - even earlier centuries. Ancient cars from bygone days still roamed the city, held together by little more than the hopes and prayers of their owners. The Santo Expedito International Airport received three flights a day: one from Kingston, one from Havana, and one from Rio.

Politics was another unchanging aspect of life on Cabrito. Since he was first elected in 1956, Francisco Rabelo had enjoyed the unwavering support of the island's elite family. Consequently, he felt no need to invest in Cabrito's decaying infrastructure. Instead, he devoted himself heart and soul to the building of his personal fortune at the expense of the public coffers.

Then, quite unexpectedly, in an election which was supposed to have only one candidate, Rabelo found himself facing vigorous opposition. Leftist revolutionary Camilo Saraiva - purportedly funded by Cuba - had somehow obtained very specific information about the current administration's systematic plundering of public funds. Undaunted by the refusal of the nation's only newspaper, *A Verdade,* to publish his findings, Saraiva ran off thousands of copies on a mimeograph machine and posted them on walls and light posts throughout the capital.

Now, for the first time in his career as a "public servant," Rabelo found himself obliged to think about serving the public. Desperate, he looked around for some area of infrastructure that he could modernize at minimum cost and maximum publicity for himself. He settled on the public telephone system.

Woefully antiquated and decrepit, the pay phones had been neither updated nor repaired since the Fifties. With uncharacteristic zeal, Rabelo set to work. He contracted an American company and bought millions of dollars worth of equipment. The new phones that sprouted up around the island had the words "Alô Cabrito" stenciled on them in white letters. Underneath were the words "Adm. F. Rabelo," so nobody would forget who was responsible for such a giant technological leap forward.

"My fellow Cabritanos," he began in his weekly radio address, "my opponent has accused me of trying to buy your votes with the *Alô Cabrito* project. I want to assure you that nothing could be further from the truth. After all, if I were just trying to get votes, why would I put a public phone in the Ipuna Jungle, for the Indians to use? I give you my word, I only have in mind the modernization of my beloved Cabrito."

There it was: he had promised to build a public phone for the Indians. And, in a move totally out of character for Rabelo, he set out immediately to fulfill his promise. The American contractors hired for the task scratched their heads at the idea. Why would anybody put a pay phone in the jungle? But, as the compensation was generous, they shrugged their shoulders and ran the underground line from the nearest substation into the rainforest.

Meanwhile, Rabelo ordered the military to find a suitable Indian village. The helicopters finally located a group of thatched dwellings not too far into the dense jungle, and the contractors dutifully laid the cables and installed the phone. The aluminum post and blue fiberglass cover presented a stark contrast to the thatched huts of the Yamani tribe.

It was just this kind of contrast that Francisco Rabelo was looking for. This would symbolize to the people of Cabrito that his administration - no, that *he* - represented progress from the Stone Age to the modern world.

The inauguration of the *telefone dos índios* was a grand affair. Rabelo brought out a camera crew from Cabrito's only TV station, together with as many reporters and photographers as he could round up. With a handful of Yamani Indians standing by, he made an inspiring speech about how these phones would unite all

Cabritanos in one big, happy family. Then, with great ceremony, he placed a token in the slot and slowly, dramatically, punched in a number.

At the presidential palace in Santo Expedito, another gaggle of reporters and photographers waited in a large state room. Before them was an oaken table on which sat a telephone. At the table, facing those assembled, sat Osvaldo Ferraz, loyal and ambitious Secretary of State for the Rabelo administration.

On cue, the phone let out two short rings, followed by a pause and then two more short rings. Osvaldo picked up the phone.

"*Alô, senhor Presidente.*" There was a round of applause from the reporters, and the photographers strained to get a good shot of the event. It was the first phone call from an Indian village to the presidential palace.

It was also the last.

As the election drew near, the ruling family of Cabrito at last came to Rabelo's aid, and through strong-arm tactics and voter fraud the incumbent was duly declared the victor. Camilo Saraiva and his auxiliaries melted into the jungle, never to be heard from again. Some theorized darkly that he had been assassinated. The official version, promoted vigorously by *A Verdade,* was that he had been evacuated to Cuba in the dead of night by a Russian submarine.

Whatever the fate of his opponent, Rabelo's victory celebration was short-lived. In his enthusiasm for the *Alô Cabrito* program, he had failed to take a few important details into consideration.

One such detail was that the Yamani Indians are a migratory tribe. They stay in one place for about a month and then leave in search of better hunting. Hence, even if they had possessed the necessary tokens to operate "their" pay phone, and even if they had possessed any reason whatsoever to call anybody in the capital city, and even if they had understood the meaning of the markings on the ten little buttons, they would not have been able to take it with them when they moved, which they did two days after the election.

Perhaps the *presidente* would have been gratified to know that, sensing something important was connected to the phone, the Yamanis returned regularly for about a year afterward to adorn it with flowers and leave gifts at its aluminum base.

But he would not have had much time to revel in that fact. Another detail he failed to take into account was Osvaldo Ferraz, his loyal and ambitious Secretary of State. Ferraz, it turns out, was much more ambitious than he was loyal. The military *coup* that would signal the end of the Rabelo administration took place a mere two days after the election results were made public.

And so, as the Yamani Indians made their way to their new dwelling place, they paused briefly to gawk at the twin-prop airplane carrying *ex*-president Francisco Rabelo to his "mandatory retirement" in Brazil.

Meanwhile, back in Santo Expedito, jubilant crowds flooded the streets and tore apart anything that would remind them of the Rabelo administration - including every last one of the brand-new public phones.

CHAPTER 1

HELLO...GOODBYE!

Twenty-seven years later, the Santo Expedito International Airport still received only three flights a day: Havana, Kingston, and Rio. At two in the afternoon on Friday, October 25, 2013, the Kingston flight touched down and taxied to a stop. As the propellers were winding down, attendants pushed an aluminum stairway to the plane. The door opened with a *hiss*, and Maxwell Sherman - Max, to his friends - stepped out into the bright sunlight.

Pausing briefly at the top of the stairs, the tall, solidly-built American got his first real look at the island. Beyond the low buildings of the airport, he could see the chaotic skyline of Santo Expedito and beyond that, the green, mist-shrouded peak which the natives called *Dedo de Deus* - God's Finger.

"So this is Cabrito," he muttered to himself. As he descended the staircase, the tropical climate brought back to his mind unwanted memories of other jungle climes, memories he tried in vain to erase.

This will be nothing like the old days, he reassured himself. *Just a simple construction project to help some missionaries.*

Max was one of exactly fifteen passengers arriving from Kingston, so it took no time for him to get through customs - no visa required, just pay a fee and stamp the passport - and pick up his baggage, which consisted of a small suitcase and a backpack. Packed inside were enough clothes to last two weeks, assorted tools, a couple of books to read in his spare time, and a variety of toys. These last were gifts for two little boys Max had never met: Justin and Tyler Blake.

Max put his suitcase down and surveyed his surroundings. His eyes scanned the single corridor of airport, which was lined with souvenir shops and small *bodegas*. A number of people milled about, but Max was looking for the Blakes, who were nowhere to be seen.

Nothing to do but wait, he concluded. A row of plastic chairs divided the corridor from one end to the other, so Max went over to them and sat down. As he tried in vain to make himself comfortable, his mind wandered back to what had brought him to this point.

It was cool Sunday morning in upstate New York about three months earlier. The sun was shining through the stained-glass windows of the Greensborough Community Church. The building itself hearkened back to pre-Civil War days: wooden floor, wooden walls, wooden pews - the ornate wooden roof was no longer visible due to the recent installation of a drop-ceiling. While it drastically reduced the heating costs, this new addition had the unfortunate effect of cutting off about a third of the ancient stained-glass panes. Thus, in the window nearest to Max, a headless Mary sat next to a headless and shoulder-less Joseph, cuddling the Baby Jesus, who was, thankfully, intact. Beneath the window, on a copper plaque, were the names of a couple - long since forgotten - who had donated the funds for the window art. Max doubted if Colonel and Mrs. Jedediah Rucker would be pleased with the sanctuary's new look.

At the front of the auditorium, Pastor Dave was talking to the organist. Max fidgeted in the uncomfortable pew, anxious for the service to start. He stole a furtive glance at the girl next to him. Mary Sue Perkins, his girlfriend of three years, was sitting with her parents, Tom and Fran. Her head was bowed, eyes closed. Her hands were folded over her Bible, which was open on her lap. *So spiritual,* Max thought. *Praying before the service. Why didn't I think of that?*

He picked up the bulletin in his lap and opened it. Inserted between the order of service and the list of ushers and nursery workers for the coming month was a letter from the Blakes, missionaries to Cabrito.

Max had only a vague idea of where Cabrito was. His travels, though surprisingly extensive for a young man of thirty-four, had never taken him to the tiny archipelago. He had seen a couple of letters from the Blakes, however, and was familiar with their work. They were people who sacrificed so much, going with their two young boys to work on a remote island that didn't even have internet! As he read the letter, a sentence jumped out at him.

"*We are praying for experienced construction workers to come to Cabrito and help us put up a new church building.*"

Construction. He could do that. "Construction worker" was just one of the hats he had worn in his short but eventful life. Excitedly, he nudged Mary Sue. She frowned and closed her eyes even tighter. The message was clear: *I'm praying, and you should be, too.*

Dutifully, Max closed his eyes, but in his mind he was already planning his trip to Cabrito. He would be the answer to the Blakes' prayers!

Now, three months later, here he was. Pastor Dave had been thrilled with Max's decision. He had been discipling Max since his conversion to Christianity four years prior, and felt that Max needed to be involved in a ministry that would provide a challenge for him.

Mary Sue, while less enthusiastic, finally agreed that it would be "an opportunity for Max to grow." Max was especially grateful to hear this because the word "growth" - as in, Max's need for it - came up regularly whenever their conversations turned to marriage.

The flight from JFK to Miami had been comfortable. Miami to Kingston, less so. Kingston to Santo Expedito had been pure torture. Now, squirming on the hard plastic seat in the airport lobby, Max wondered where his hosts were. Mr. Blake had assured him that he would be waiting to meet him when he arrived. Max looked at his watch. Forty-five minutes, and still no missionary.

Wonder if he's waiting outside, Max thought. He stood up, slung his backpack over his shoulder, picked up his suitcase, and set out toward the main entrance. On the way, he passed the darkened window of a closed establishment. He paused and shook his head at the reflection looking back at him. His unruly, sandy-red hair had reminded more than one person of his distant relative - that bellicose Civil War commander who was at once the toast of the North and the bane of Georgia. Like General Sherman, Max Sherman's eyes were a piercing blue. Separated by generations, the two Shermans—William Tecumseh and Max--also shared a hardness to their features born by hard experiences. The similarities ended there, however. The wiry, notoriously homely, temperamentally unpleasant general was a far cry from the fit, attractive, good-natured Max.

Leaning closer to the darkened window, he examined the five-o'clock shadow that had formed on his well-defined jaw-line during his flight.

Mom would be mortified if she saw that, he reflected. *Come to think of it, so would Mary Sue.*

Suddenly, there was a bustle of activity from the other end of the long corridor. A portly, balding man was making his way rapidly toward the gate. Trailing behind him were a frazzled wife, two small boys, and a native porter, pulling a cart that was groaning under a load of suitcases. Putting his own suitcases down, Max pulled out the photo and looked at it, and then at the approaching family. It was them, alright, although they did not look anywhere near as polished in real life.

"Mr. Blake!"

To his surprise, the missionary went right by without even turning his head. Max ran to catch up.

"Mr. Blake! It's me, Maxwell Sherman. I'm here to help with the construction, remember?"

The missionary stopped and looked at Max for a moment with a blank expression on his face. Then his eyes widened and his jaw dropped. His hand went to his forehead.

"Maxwell... oh my... that was THIS week! Oh..."

Max was confused. "What do you mean?"

"Oh, this is awkward..." stammered the missionary.

"We are leaving." The blunt explanation came from Mrs. Blake with absolute finality, as if to remove any doubt that Max's arrival might have thrown on the situation. "We are going back to the States - today." Max noted a special emphasis on the word "today."

"But... what am I supposed to do now?"

Mrs. Blake had never stopped herding the children toward the gate. "George, come on! If we miss this plane..." There was a threatening tone to her voice.

George sighed and looked at Max. "Listen, I feel so bad about this whole thing. It's just that... well... we have to go. Here..." he pulled a piece of paper and pen from his shirt pocket and began scribbling. "This is the address to our house."

Max took the paper and stared blankly at it.

"Your house…"

"We didn't have time to sell it," George explained. "You can stay there until you get a flight back. Nothing fancy, but at least it will be a roof over your head. Hopefully you can transfer your ticket and get out of here pretty quickly. Here are the keys."

"George! Come ON!" It was Mrs. Blake again.

"Coming dear! Max… once again… so sorry. Gotta go!"

And just like that, he was gone. Fifteen minutes later, Max watched as their plane, the same plane that had brought him from Kingston, took off and disappeared into the clouds. Slowly the shock began to wear off, and Max's mind began to work on solutions.

"Next flight out," he muttered to himself. He turned around to where he had seen the ticket counter for the airline. It was closed.

"It's Friday afternoon." The American-sounding voice came from behind him. "All the ticket agencies are closed till Monday."

Max turned to see an older man dressed in faded jeans and a tank top. He had a scraggly grey beard and wore a much-used canvas hat. Piercing gray eyes peered at Max from under the rim. Max couldn't tell right away how old he was. Fifty? Sixty, perhaps? The man stepped forward and extended his hand. Max shook it firmly.

"Raymond Sand," he said. "Folks here call me *Raimundo*. To Americans, I'm just Ray." He nodded in the general direction of the departing plane. "Seems our family of *gringos* had about all they could take of Cabrito."

"Did you know them?"

"We were acquainted. Americans overseas tend to gravitate to other Americans. I just brought them from their home in my cab."

"You're a cabbie?"

"I prefer 'transportation professional,'" said the older man with a wide grin. "I do a lot of things - 'cabbie' just happens to be my profession *du jour*. And since it looks like you're going to be here for the weekend…"

"I'll be needing a ride," completed Max, somewhat wearily.

Ray grinned. "My rates are competitive. Cash only, of course, but I accept all major currencies."

"That settles it," said Max. He was already beginning to like the man.

"In that case, let me help you with your bag."

With that, the two men walked out into the hot Cabritan sun. Ray led the way to a decrepit-looking yellow Volkswagen beetle parked by the curb at the entrance to the airport. A boy in ragged shorts loitered by the curb. Ray fished through his pockets.

"You don't happen to have a coin on you," he wondered. "This little guy has been 'guarding' my car, and expects to be paid." The boy looked up at him and smiled expectantly. Max fished around in his pocket and produced an American quarter. He flipped it to the boy, who caught it deftly in the air.

"*Obrigado, senhor!*" the boy said, examining the shiny coin.

"*De nada,*" Max replied.

Hearing the Portuguese, Ray cocked his head and looked at his new acquaintance. Max shrugged.

"Crash course." he explained as he entered the taxi.

Tired from his long trip and perplexed by his present situation, Max did not pay any attention to the tall, thin-faced soldier in the olive uniform and De Gaul-style cap, who was standing by the air-port entrance. The soldier, however, paid close attention to Max. He puffed casually on a cigarette and watched through half-closed eyes as the two Americans left, then threw his cigarette on the ground and strode off toward a waiting car.

CHAPTER 2

THE NEED FOR SPEED

aymond's taxi - or *Transporte Raimundo*, as the letters emblazoned on the side announced to the world - was actually just an aged yellow Volkswagen Beetle that looked like it had been through at least one war. As they got in, Max found himself having serious doubts as to its structural integrity.

Ray put his key into the ignition and, miraculously, the decrepit VW coughed to life. Without warning, Ray punched the gas. The car lurched forward with a vengeance, momentarily pinning Max's head against the seat. With tires squealing, they shot out of the parking lot and began a frenetic race through the streets of Santo Expedito.

"These islands were discovered by the Portuguese back in the early sixteenth century," began Raymond, his matter-of-fact tone contrasting with his haphazard driving.

Max looked around for a seatbelt - there was none.

"They set up a small colony, and that is why Portuguese is the official language - although most folks speak a kind of hybrid language they call *Kryollo*. It's a combination of Portuguese and a slew of native and African tribal dialects."

The yellow taxi cut off another vehicle in order to make a left turn. Max suspected that the driver of the other car was using the most colorful words from all those dialects.

Ray continued, unfazed. "The Portuguese high-and-mighties never paid much mind to this God-forsaken rock. It became a hideout for pirates, escaped convicts, and the like from all over the world. So while the main culture is *latino*, there is a pretty healthy ethnic mix going way back."

"I'm not familiar with the word 'Cabrito'. What does that mean?" Max asked wondering if it might not mean "taxi drivers from Hell."

"Means 'kid', as in, a baby goat. The first critters the Portuguese explorers saw when they landed were a kind of small wild goat that lives here. They gave it the name *Ilha dos Cabritos* - Goat Island. Later it got shortened to just 'Cabrito'. The group of smaller islands that surround us are called the Cabritanas. You have to admit, the Portuguese language makes it sound much more romantic."

"How many people live here?" Max wanted to know. He was fully convinced that by the time they reached their destination, there would be a few less. In rounding the last corner, they had actually driven *on the sidewalk*.

"That's kind of hard to tell. The official census reads about two million, but they really have no way of counting the Indians that live in the Ipuna jungle to the northwest. They keep pretty much to themselves. I think…"

Ray had to stop talking in order to slam on the brakes as a long, black Rolls-Royce barreled across a narrow intersection in front of them. There were two police motorcycles in front of the car and twelve strung out behind. All had sirens blaring.

"What was that?" Max asked when the procession had passed.

"A rare treat," said Ray with a grunt. "You just got a glimpse of *the* Osvaldo Ferraz, *presidente* of Cabrito. Or, at least, a glimpse of his car."

"That was quite the motorcade."

"Yeah, well, he is very fond of the trappings, real big on pomp and ceremony." It was not hard to notice the disgust in Ray's voice.

"You've met him?"

"Once or twice." The Volkswagen lurched back into action. "I try to keep a low profile," Ray grunted. "Being an American, that's not always easy. But Ferraz is mostly show. The real power on this island lies in the Santana family - George Santana, to be specific."

"*The* George Santana?" Max asked, incredulous. "The multi-billionaire George Santana? The guy who manipulates the world stock markets at will and funds all those 'nonprofit political action groups' in the US?"

"One and the same."

"I had no idea he was from here."

"Cabrito, born and bred. Of course, we don't see too much of him. He's too busy jet-setting all over the globe to trouble himself with the affairs of the island he practically owns. Instead, he delegates affairs here to his son, Emídio. And that is one dangerous *hombre*. If you have any knack for survival at all you'll stay right away from that guy."

Max knew that his chances of ever coming into contact with Emídio Santana were slim to none. He was curious about one thing, however.

"So what's your story? How does a guy from the US end up on Cabrito, driving a taxi?" Max used the word "driving" in its loosest possible sense.

There was a long pause before Ray answered. "Back in the Eighties, I found it necessary to relocate," he replied. "I came here with an outfit that was putting in a telephone system. Ended up staying. I like it here, and I manage to keep my head above water."

Max found it easy to like the older man. Despite his driving habits, which Max noticed were far from unique on Cabrito, the man had an easygoing, laid-back way about him. *Probably because he has been out of the US for so long,* Max mused.

"I've always liked cars," the old man continued. Max would never have guessed, based on the way his new acquaintance was treating the poor VW. "Here on Cabrito it's easy to find old cars, and I get a kick out of fixing them up. Have quite a collection at my place. Got a '57 Chevy, a '39 Mercedes, and a few others. If you were staying longer, I'd show you."

"If you have all those cars, why don't you drive one of them around town instead of this beat up old Beetle?"

"Are you kidding? Have you *seen* the way people drive around here?" Without showing the least hint of irony, or slowing, Ray made a sharp turn and entered the narrow passageway of an open-air market.

"The *feira*," commented Ray, as a terrified chicken sprinted out of the way. An instant's hesitation, and it would have been flattened. "It's Friday afternoon: shopping time."

After successfully navigating the obstacle course of fruit and vegetable stands and narrowly missing a host of assorted livestock, the taxi made a right-hand turn and entered what appeared to be a residential area. Nearly identical houses painted in pastel colors were packed in tightly together on either side of the winding cobblestone road. The car made several twists and turns, with every new street looking just like the last one.

"So what brings *you* to Cabrito, Max?" his driver asked as he carefully maneuvered between two pigs that were claiming joint ownership of the road.

Max summarized the events that had led him to the island nation.

"So you're not another missionary."

The way Ray pronounced the word "missionary" gave Max to believe that his companion had little respect for that particular subset of humanity.

"I guess not. Are there many of them here?"

"None, as of about an hour ago. There have been several since I arrived, but they never seem to have much staying power. I pick them up at the airport, all fresh-faced and talking about how God sent them here. Then, a few months later, I take them back."

Max pondered this for a moment. What was it about Cabrito, other than crazy drivers, that was so hard on missionaries? Finally, he turned to Ray. "Well, I'm afraid I'm going to last even less time. You can take me back to the airport as soon as it opens on Monday."

Ray chuckled. "So I take it you aren't particularly religious?"

"I'm a believer in Christ, if that's what you mean."

As if to accentuate the need for a home in the hereafter, the cab made a turn so severe that Max felt sure it would tip over on its side. He gripped the door handle and continued, "I've been a believer for about four years. I'm just under no delusion that I should be a missionary in Cabrito. I came here to help out with a construction project, that's all."

Ray flashed another of his infectious grins. "Sounds religious to me," he said. The taxi clipped the corner of a vendor's cart, sending fruits and vegetables flying in all directions. The curses of the poor merchant faded quickly into the background.

"And you?" Max asked.

"Me?" the older man shook his head. "I think it's a bunch of nonsense. My only religion is 'survival of the fittest.'" Ray turned toward his passenger, and in doing so, did not see the speed bump that he was rapidly approaching. The little taxi went airborne, and then came back to earth with a jarring thud.

"Sounds good, as long as you happen to be the fittest," observed Max, not at all convinced that he was going to survive this ride.

"It's worked for me so far."

They continued on in silence for a while, until the taxi made another sharp right-hand turn - the little car went up on two wheels during the maneuver - and started up a steep hill. As they gained altitude, Max noticed that the size and quality of the dwellings were beginning to increase. Presently, they found themselves in a neighborhood of large houses surrounded by imposing brick walls, many with barbed wire and shards of glass ringing the top. Ray swung the taxi onto a side road and stopped in front of a solid metal gate. Max breathed a sigh of relief.

"This is the place," announced Ray.

After extracting himself from the cab - he resisted the urge to drop to his knees and kiss the ground - Max began trying keys in the gate. On the third key, it swung open, revealing a manicured courtyard with a stone path that meandered up to the porch of a modest - by American standards - two-story, white-stucco house. Ray got out and brought Max's suitcases to him.

"It might not look like much, but compared to how most people here live, this is the Ritz."

"It looks fine," said Max. As he turned to get his bags, he noticed a man approaching. The newcomer looked to be in his mid-forties: dark-skinned, somewhat round in the middle, and balding. He came up to Max and started speaking. Max glanced at Ray.

"Kryollo?"

"Yep. He says he wants to know what you are doing here. His name is Bernardinho. Says he attends the church the Blakes started."

"Can you fill him in on my, ah, situation?"

Ray turned to the diminutive islander and spoke to him in fluid Kryollo. The man paid close attention and then turned to Max and spoke again.

"Says he's glad you're here. He will make sure your stay is comfortable. He says he was saddened by the missionaries leaving, but is happy you are going to take their place."

"No, you don't understand," protested Max at once. "I can't stay. I'm only going to be here a couple of days. Explain that to him."

Ray did, and a sad expression came across Bernardinho's face. He turned to Max and spoke. "You come to my house." He indicated a house two blocks down. "You eat with my family. We talk. Seven o'clock." Then he turned and shuffled back down the road.

Ray helped Max with his suitcase and then headed back to his taxi. Max followed him.

"How much do I owe you?" he asked.

"A ten-spot should cover it." Max handed him the money. In return, Ray pressed a rather smudged business card into Max's hand. "I know you are leaving on Monday, but if you should happen to need anything, give me a call."

"Thanks for all your help," replied Max, putting the card in his wallet. "I don't know what I would have done if you hadn't been there." Then, remembering a message Pastor Dave had preached not long ago about divine appointments, he added, "God had you in the right place at the right time."

"God… luck… karma… whatever." With a dismissive wave, Ray got into his taxi. The yellow Volkswagen coughed to life and rattled down the road.

Max watched him go, then turned back to the house, closing the gate behind him. A manicured green yard surrounded the simple yet attractive house. He walked up the stone pathway to the porch, opened the door, and went inside.

Max found himself in a spacious living area furnished with an easy-chair, a couch, and a TV. Apparently, the Blakes had not even had time to dispose of their furniture. To the right was a dining area and the kitchen. A circular metal staircase wound its way up to the second floor. Upon climbing it, Max found two bedrooms - both fully furnished - and an office. A few books had been hurriedly grabbed from the shelves, but other than that, the office looked untouched.

They must have been in a big hurry to leave, Max thought to himself. Suddenly, he felt very tired. He went downstairs, picked up his bags, and then climbed back up to the master bedroom. Before flopping onto the bed, he opened his carry-on bag and took out a small framed picture of a smiling blond girl with rosy cheeks, dressed in a denim jumper. She had written *Love forever, Mary Sue* on the front with red ink, followed by a series of small hearts. Next to these was a Bible reference: Proverbs 3:5-6. Looking at his sweetheart's image, he smiled.

Just a few days, he thought, as he stretched out on the bed. *I'll see what there is to see here in Cabrito and be back in your arms before I know it.* He placed the picture on the stand beside the bed and was soon fast asleep.

After the close encounter with the yellow taxi, the black Rolls Royce continued its breakneck romp through the streets of Santo Expedito - accompanied always by the motorcycle entourage - until it pulled up to a foreboding black iron gate. The gate swung open to reveal a large manicured lawn, divided evenly in half by a palm-lined driveway, which led straight to the presidential mansion. Actually, *mansion* was an understatement. The official residence of the *presidente* of Cabrito was the very definition of opulence. It was called the *casa branca* - or White House. But what the Cabritan government lacked in originality when it came to choosing a name, they made up for in the "fancy" department. Marble floors, golden fixtures, crystal chandeliers - no expense had been spared to say to the world "only the best for the *presidente* of Cabrito."

That the same did not apply to the majority of Cabrito's populace was an inconsistency the *presidente* did not spend much time worrying about, especially now.

Inside the limousine, Osvaldo Ferraz smiled. In his thirty years as *presidente*, he had never tired of the trappings of power. He loved how people fell over themselves to carry out his smallest whim, how uniformed guards opened the gate and saluted at his arrival, how his limousine - specially customized in England and presented to him as a gift by George Santana himself at his inauguration - made all the smaller cars on the island scurry for side streets. Not bad for a kid from the slums.

The long driveway led to the entrance of the presidential mansion, with its oaken doors, Greek columns, and sculpted trimmings. The limousine stopped there, and a soldier materialized to open the door. President Ferraz stepped out and gave a casual salute. He was met on the porch by his *chargé d'affaires*, a portly man named Borges, who seemed to be constantly sweating.

"Good afternoon, *senhor Presidente*."

Ferraz barely acknowledged the greeting and started walking towards the large double doors in long, deliberate strides - the gait of a man in charge. Borges kept talking.

"Everything is all set for the gala tomorrow night."

"Good."

"The invited guests have all indicated that they will be in attendance."

"Excellent." They were now inside the mansion, climbing the grand staircase that led to the second floor.

"Diego called about fifteen minutes ago."

"And is everything in order on that front?"

"Yes, the birds have flown… so to speak."

"Perfect."

"Indeed." The two men were at the top of the stairway, and Borges had paused to catch his breath and wipe his perpetually moist forehead. "Dr. Santana will be very pleased."

Ferraz wheeled around to glare at his secretary. "This has nothing to do with what Santana wants! *I* am president of this country. *I* make the decisions. The *gringos* had to leave because *I* decided they had to leave. Do I make myself clear?"

"Crystal clear." Borges wiped a dab of sweat from his brow.

The president's composure returned. "Now, what is next on the agenda?"

"There is someone in your office to see you."

"Who?"

"Santana."

Ferraz blanched. "*Meu Deus!* Santana is in my office? Why didn't you tell me? Just… wait here." He half-turned, then turned back. "How do I look? Do I look alright?"

"You look very… presidential, *senhor*."

If Ferraz noted the sarcasm in his secretary's voice, he made no sign of it. Instead, he took a deep breath and timidly opened the door to his office. A tall man was standing inside, inspecting one of the paintings on the wall. He was dressed in a perfectly tailored business suit, holding a pair of reading glasses in his hand. Upon the entrance of the *presidente*, he turned and fixed his clear-blue eyes upon him.

"Good afternoon, *senhor Presidente*." There was no mistaking the irony in the way he spoke the title.

"Good afternoon, Dr. Santana. What a pleasant surprise. I do hope *dona* Francesca is well and…"

"Let us not waste time with useless pleasantries," interrupted the taller man. He spoke with a cool authority that made Osvaldo Ferraz shut his mouth mid-word. "I will get straight to the point.

I am somewhat concerned about the gala planned for tomorrow evening."

"Did you not get an invitation? I am sure they were…"

"Of course I did." Again the cool interruption. "What bothers me most is that this little celebration of yours is in honor of the new director of our National Foundation for Indigenous Policy." Santana stopped and looked at the chief executive, as if he should understand the significance of that remark.

"Sir?" Ferraz did not understand.

Santana sighed and continued. "As you well know, there is a big place in my heart for the Indian races on our little island. The relationship of the Santana family with our brown brothers has always been… special. And our indigenous policy is very effective at preserving them in their pristine, uncorrupted state. One of the reasons that it is so effective, is that it is *not publicized*."

"Of course, Dr. Santana. A very wise policy indeed."

"So then why are we holding a big, publicized *baile* for the new director?"

"Well… it…" Ferraz was at a loss. "It seemed like a good idea…" he finished weakly. "I will cancel it at once."

Santana rolled his eyes. "No, canceling the event now would call more attention to it. Here is what we will do. As you know, the Santana family has been in negotiations with an American firm to open a factory here in Santo Expedito. This will bring jobs and economic growth to Cabrito."

As well as certain financial benefits to the Santana family, Ferraz thought, wisely keeping his thoughts to himself.

"These negotiations are very important to my father. Hence, the gala will be in honor of their company representative, who has just arrived. During the event we will announce the new director of indigenous policy, which should show our American friend that we are a 'culturally sensitive' people. Americans are easily impressed by that sort of thing."

"What an excellent idea!" enthused Osvaldo Ferraz, hoping his insincerity was not as evident to Santana as it was to him. "I will instruct the planners to make the necessary adjustments to the program."

"I expect nothing less." Santana paused and turned to the painting he had been examining. "Do you know what this painting depicts, *senhor Presidente*?"

"Of course. It shows the landing of the Portuguese on Cabrito."

"Right you are." Dr. Santana beamed at him in a gratingly patronizing way. "My family commissioned this painting over a hundred years ago. It is based on eyewitness accounts. And do you see this man right here?"

Osvaldo squinted to see where Santana was pointing with his glasses.

"This man is my direct ancestor, Teófilo Santana. He was one of the first men to step ashore of the island."

The man in the painting bore an uncanny resemblance to Dr. Santana. His sword was drawn, and he was pointing it at a group of Yamani tribesmen who were cowering a short distance away. Ferraz identified with the Yamanis more than he wanted to admit.

"The point is. . ." Dr. Santana continued. The *presidente* was pretty sure he knew what the point was. "The point is that the Santana family has been influential on this island for a long, long time. Presidents have come and presidents have gone…" Osvaldo Ferraz cringed at the word "gone." "…but we have always been here. And we always will be."

"Yes, Dr. Santana. I understand perfectly."

"I hope you do. Our working relationship over the last three decades has been… convenient. Remember, my father placed you in office just as he handed over the administration of his affairs here to me. Since that time, you and I have accomplished much together. You have been a very useful…." he paused.

Lackey? Stooge? Boot-licker? Ferraz' mind filled in the blank space with no prompting.

"…associate. It would be a shame to see something regrettable happen now. I am still uneasy about this gala. Make sure nothing goes wrong."

Ferraz desperately wanted to change the subject. Suddenly he remembered. "Dr. Santana, I am pleased to report that the American missionaries have left the island."

Santana looked at him with something resembling pity. "Of course, I already know this. I also know that as they were leaving, another arrived."

Ferraz's brow furrowed in consternation. This was something new. Why had Diego not told him of this?

"Please do your best to make sure that this new arrival follows his compatriots as soon as possible. You may leave now."

So eager was *presidente* Osvalso Ferraz to get out of that conversation, that only later did it dawn on him that Santana had dismissed him from his own office.

CHAPTER 3

The afternoon nap did Max a world of good. Upon awaking, he showered (he had seen electric shower heads before and had always wondered about the advisability of mixing electrical currents with water), shaved, and made a valiant attempt at putting some order to his unruly mop of red hair. He chose a fresh pair of jeans and a polo shirt from his suitcase. Brown loafers completed the ensemble.

In the living room, he picked up the remote control and briefly flipped through the channels on TV. Brazilian *novelas*, soccer games, and infomercials badly dubbed into Cabritan Portuguese - nothing that made him want to sit down and watch. Max turned the TV off and was about to explore the bookshelves in the study when he heard a light tapping sound on the metal gate outside.

It was Bernardinho, accompanied this time by a girl of fourteen or fifteen years. She had short, black hair done up with a bow, and she was wearing what appeared to be a school uniform. "My daughter, Isabel," he said by way of introduction. "She speak English very good."

"I'm pleased to meet you," said Max, holding out his hand.

Isabel extended her own hand shyly. "I'm please to meet you, too, Mister Missionary Max."

"It's just Max," corrected the American.

"I am sorry... just Max. You come eat with us now."

Perhaps it was because he had not eaten a decent meal in two days, or perhaps it was the newness of Cabritan culinary arts on his tongue. Whatever it was, Max was certain he had never tasted better food than what was set before him by Luciene, Bernadinho's wife. A large, jolly woman whose grey-speckled hair was pulled back severely to a bun, she hovered over Max like a mother hen, constantly asking - through her daughter - if he liked what he was eating and if he wanted more. When he tried to refuse seconds, she concluded, loudly, that it was because he didn't like the food. Max took seconds.

And thirds.

Meanwhile, he was peppered with questions having to do with his nationality. (Yes, he had been to New York City, Hollywood and Las Vegas. No, he had never met Michael Jordan.) Finally, a very full Max retired with the family to the small living room, where Bernardinho began to fill Max in on the situation of the church recently abandoned by the Blakes. He spoke in Kryollo, while his daughter tested the outer limits of her English.

"*Pode falar em português, se quiser,*" Max said helpfully. "You can speak in Portuguese if you wish."

Bernandinho's eyes lit up. "You speak Portuguese?" he asked, slipping easily into the official language of his homeland. "Where did you learn it?

Max shrugged. *"Curso de imersão,"* he replied. "Crash course."

Bernardinho raised his eyebrows as if to say *That must have been some crash course,* but then began again with his narration of the events leading up to Max's presence.

"Things were going well. People were coming to our little church, and we were getting ready to enlarge our building to be able to fit them all."

"That's why I'm here," said Max. "I came to help the Blakes with the construction."

Bernardinho nodded. "We heard about you, and we were praying for you."

Max felt this was the time to ask a question that had been burning in his mind. "What was it that made the Blakes leave in such a hurry? I mean, they didn't even get rid of their things."

His host shook his head sadly. "I do not know. One day we make plans for the future of the church, the next day he tells me they have to leave. And then the next day, they are gone!"

"That would be today," Max muttered to himself. To his host he asked, "Where is the church?"

"It is in this neighborhood, not too far away. On Sunday you go with us. You can speak to our congregation."

That proposition alarmed Max to no small degree. Him? Speak? He tried to protest, but Bernardinho would hear nothing of it. "You are sent by American church, you will speak to us on Sunday."

Max was not sure how being American made him qualified to preach in a church on Cabrito, but he could tell there would be no getting around it. Perhaps he could find something interesting in one of the books at the Blake residence - or rather, the *former* Blake residence.

For the rest of the evening, Max listened as Bernardinho and his family told him about the Cabritana islands. He could not help but be fascinated by their colorful history and intrigued by the way this family seemed very proud of their heritage. Finally, Bernardinho stood up and spoke.

"It's getting late," he said. "You should go home and rest. I will go with you."

"Oh, that's not necessary," replied the young American. "I can make it there on my own."

Bernardinho looked doubtful. "Please be careful. The streets of Santo Expedito can be very dangerous at night." Assuring them that he would take no unnecessary risks, he left, but not before *dona* Luciene gave him a bag of food and urged him to return as often as he would like for meals.

As he stepped out into the warm night air, Max got the distinct impression that somebody, somewhere, was watching him. He looked around and, seeing nobody, shrugged and started down the street.

Closer... closer... Cascavel, "rattlesnake," fingered the switchblade in his hand as he watched the *americano* climb the hill. He was a man who enjoyed his work. The money was okay, but the part he loved was that moment when surprise turned to fear, and then fear to absolute terror and panic.

Closer... He licked his lips in anticipation. *NOW!*

Cascavel jumped out in front of the American. *"Passa a grana, ou eu furo você!"* Then, showing off for his obviously foreign victim, "Give me money!"

The *bandido* waited for the fear and panic to take over. But to his disappointment, the American looked him straight in the eyes and cocked his head to one side. Frustrated, and a little flustered at this unexpected response, Cascavel waved the knife in his victim's face.

"Money!" he shouted. "All money!"

The *americano* slowly raised his left hand - still holding the bag of food. "Okay, okay," he said soothingly. "I'm getting my wallet, see?"

With his right hand, he reached back and pulled his billfold from his jeans pocket. The mugger's eyes gleamed in anticipation. The American held it out, and then, just as Cascavel was reaching for it, he flicked his wrist to the right. The wallet flew from his hand. Instinctively, the *bandido* grabbed at it. Too late, he realized he had made a grave mistake, for as he reached for the wallet, the man in front of him exploited his temporary unbalance. The man's hand snaked out, took hold of Cascavel's wrist, and twisted the knife out of his hand. At the same time, the *bandido* felt his legs being kicked out from under him.

Cascavel landed heavily, face down. The knife clattered on the cobblestone road, just out of reach. The young American stepped on it, then bent down to pick it up. He flipped it around a few times in his hand, as if testing its balance.

The street thug known as Rattlesnake felt an unfamiliar emotion creeping into him - panic. What was going to happen now? What terrible things would this strange man do to him?

From this sprawled position on the ground, Cascavel looked up to see his would-be victim casually walk over to where the wallet lay and pick it up. Then, to his great amazement, the man opened it and took out a ten-dollar bill. Walking back to where the fallen attacker lay, the American let the paper bill fall directly in front of Cascavel's face. Then he held up the knife and took aim.

Cascavel closed his eyes. This was it. He was going to die.

Thwack! He heard the sound but felt nothing. Slowly, he opened his eyes. The knife was sticking in the ground in front of him, piercing straight through the middle of the ten-dollar bill, right between Alexander Hamilton's eyes. The americano looked at the bandido again, a wry smile playing about the man's lips. Then he deliberately turned his back and walked away.

Cascavel lay there for a few moments. The idea of grabbing the knife and heaving it at the American played through his head, but he discarded it immediately. Who knew what other tricks this man had up his sleeve? Slowly he got up, pulled his switchblade out of the ground, stuffed the money in his pocket, and slunk into the darkness.

In the shadows on the other side of the street, unseen by either of the men, Raymond Sand rubbed his jaw thoughtfully, then turned and walked back down the hill to where the yellow Volkswagen was parked.

CHAPTER 4

THE GREEN MONKEY

Max arrived at the Blakes' house unfazed; he had faced situations in his short life much more dangerous than this evening's botched mugging. He did wonder, however, if he had done the right thing. Should he have reacted like that? Did he make the situation worse? What was the story of the guy who had tried to mug him?

But another thought soon crowded out the exciting events of the night and instilled a terror in him that would have made his erstwhile assailant jealous.

They want me to speak in church!

He made straight for the little office, turned on the light, and began pulling random books off the shelves. Desperately, he opened volumes and scanned the contents, hoping against hope he might find something worthwhile to share with the congregation. Alas, most of the books had to do with diverse theological subjects that seemed to have little to do with the immediate needs of a small church on Cabrito.

He was beginning to despair when a hardcover volume, decidedly older than most of the other books on the shelf, caught his eye. It was the biography of a man named Adoniram Judson. He remembered Pastor Dave mentioning him, something about the hardships he faced on the mission field.

Max took the book down and began to read. Almost immediately, the story captivated him. It was the story of a young man living life for himself until God shook him up, turned him around, and sent him off as a missionary. Forgetting about his quest for something to say the next evening, Max turned page after page until exhaustion took over and he fell asleep, his head resting on the open pages of the book.

On the eastern end of Santo Expedito, across the bay from the tourist yachts and pleasure boats, sits the run-down *bairro* named *Praia Seca*. There one can find a range of seedy bars and nightclubs to fit every imaginable prurient taste. One such establishment, called *O Macaco Verde* - The Green Monkey - has a reputation for being the hangout of toughs and lowlifes, where rough-and-tumble dockworkers mix with salty sailors and outlaws of varied professional levels.

On this particular night, business was brisk. Among the cars parked under the glowing, maliciously grinning neon-green monkey sat a yellow Volkswagen with the words *Transporte Raimundo* emblazoned on the side. Its owner was inside, belly to the bar, staring at the dregs of his whiskey. He was still trying to register what he had seen earlier that evening, when he became aware of someone sitting next to him. He turned to see a thin man in an olive-colored uniform. The thin man wore a DeGaul-style cap on his head and a hard expression on his face.

"*Olá* Diego," Ray said. "Why am I not surprised to see you here?"

There was no mirth in the newcomer's yellow-tinged eyes. "There is a new *gringo* in town," he hissed. "You took him from the airport."

"Of course," Ray sighed.

"What can you tell me about him?"

"Name's Max. Came here to do some construction work with the family you... we... just scared off. I took him to the house, and as far as I know, he is planning to catch the first flight out of town." Ray decided to withhold information of the scene he had just witnessed. It was always good to play some cards close to one's vest.

If Diego suspected that the American was holding back, he did not let on. "As of now, you have a new assignment. You are to - "

"Let me guess," Ray interrupted with a heavy sigh. "I am to make sure that *senhor Gringo* does indeed leave the island as planned."

"I am glad we understand each other," purred Diego, a patronizing smile playing on his lips. The flat face, the yellow eyes, the hook nose, the mustache so thin it looked like it had been drawn on his upper lip, and above all, that grating attitude of superiority - all of these features made it a constant struggle for Ray not to haul off and punch Diego in the kisser. Instead he grunted and drained the last few drops of whiskey from his cup.

"And will the government of Cabrito be as generous to me for this assignment as they have been for others?" he asked.

Diego reached into the inside of his jacket and pulled out an envelope. He handed it to Ray. "Five hundred now, five hundred when he leaves." He stood up. "Do not disappoint," he finished in a voice that made no attempt to conceal his implied threat. Then he stiffly turned and stalked out of the dive.

Ray returned to his drink, and finding his glass empty, ordered up another one. In the background, a jukebox was blaring a raucous Garth Brooks tune. Ray was the only one in the room who could understand it, but he wasn't listening. With $500 in his pocket, it was shaping up to be a very good evening.

CHAPTER 5

CHANCE ENCOUNTER

The sunlight streamed through the office window. Momentarily disoriented, Max lifted his head, rubbed his eyes, and looked at the clock

Ten o'clock! He couldn't remember when he had slept in that late. Then again, the previous day had been eventful, to say the least.

Max looked at the book on the desk in front of him, and reflected on his reading from the previous night. There was no doubt about it, Adoniram Judson was his new hero. It was not just the fact that Judson was the first Christian missionary in Burma - and the first-ever foreign missionary from America - that impressed Max. It was how he labored hard for nine years with no converts. How he was imprisoned twice, once by the French and once by the Burmese. How he buried two wives in the Burmese soil before the third wife buried him. Obviously, the word "quit" did not exist in Judson's vocabulary. What a contrast he was to the missionary family Max had encountered yesterday at the airport beating a hasty retreat. The more he read, the more he wondered if Mr. Blake had ever cracked open this book.

Max closed the book and placed it back on the shelf. The need for food, combined with a growing feeling of being cooped up in the house, made him decide to go exploring. Having slept in his clothes, he showered, changed, and left the house, trying his best to remember the route the taxi had taken the day before.

Max's previous line of work had fine-tuned his natural sense of direction. He set off down the hill, using the taller downtown buildings as his guide, and soon found himself in the open-air market they had passed the day before.

As he walked through *feira* the vendors called out for him in Kryolle, Portuguese, or broken English, urging him to examine their wares. Max was struck by the variety of items on sale: clothing, artisan pieces, jewelry, hammocks, and an infinite number of other trinkets. Seeing a beautiful set of earrings, he thought what a nice gift they would make for Mary Sue and approached the plump woman under the awning.

"*Quanto custa?*" he asked, pointing to the earrings. Then he added, "Dollar," so she knew what the medium of exchange would be.

She grinned at him - revealing several empty spaces where teeth should have been - and held up both hands, all fingers extended. "*Dez dollar,*" she said. Then in what was probably the extent of her English, "Ten dollar... very good price."

Max was fishing for his wallet to pay the price when he heard a low female voice behind him. "I'm sure your girlfriend will be very pleased that you are paying many times what those earrings are worth. It's such a nice gesture."

Turning, Max found himself face to face with one of the most stunning creatures he had ever seen. It was as if every tropical princess from every sun-drenched island in the world had been combined into one bronze-skinned, raven-haired, dark-eyed, red-lipped, smiling vision of feminine beauty and placed in front of him. Max fiercely resisted the urge to compare the girl before him to Mary Sue, afraid of what the outcome would be if he did.

The girl stuck out her hand. "Hi! My name is Ilana." Her English was perfect, yet tinged with a slight accent that gave it an allure that Shakespeare had never dreamed of.

Ilana, Max thought, *the name is as beautiful as she is.* Then, *Get a grip, Maxwell, and say something!* "Hi." He took her hand and was surprised at the firmness of her grip. She was warm to the touch, very full of life. Suddenly, he realized that the handshake was over and he was still hanging on. Embarrassed, he let go.

Say something! his mind screamed at him. His mouth was slow in cooperating.

"You... you speak English good," he blundered. "I mean, *well...* and apparently better than I do." *Nice save.* "My name is Max."

"Well hello, Max." A small giggle let him know that she had not found his reaction to her the least bit creepy, and he wondered why he was so relieved at that. Max was no stranger to the ways of the fairer sex. Before Mary Sue, he had had many relationships of varying degrees of commitment, most of which he now looked back on with regret. He was usually self-assured around women, and yet the heavenly apparition before him was bringing back feelings he had last known in junior high.

"Would you like me to help you with the earrings?" Ilana asked him, bringing him back down to earth. *Yes, the earrings,* he thought. *The ones I am buying for Mary Sue... my girlfriend!*

"Yes, please!"

Ilana turned to the plump lady behind the counter and began to talk to her in Kryolle. When Max had heard the common tongue of Cabrito being spoken earlier, he had thought it sounded like a mixture of Spanish, German, and Farsi - languages with which he had varying degrees of familiarity. Coming from the rosy lips of Ilana, however, it sounded like sweet, sweet music.

Presently Ilana turned to him. "Two dollars," she said triumphantly. Max handed the lady two green bills, and she spoke to Ilana in Kryolle.

"What is she saying?" asked Max.

"Oh, she is thanking me for helping out."

Only someone as beautiful as this could inspire gratitude in a vendor who just took an eighty percent loss, Max mused as the lady carefully wrapped the earrings and handed them to him.

"Well, I am the one who should thank you for saving me eight bucks!"

"No problem. Glad I could help. I take it this is your first time in Cabrito."

"Is it that obvious?"

Again she giggled, and Max thought it sounded like water rippling over stones in a brook. "Always willing to help a stranger in need," she said. "Actually, I am just killing time today. Is there anything else I can help you with?"

The idea of spending more time with this marvelous creature was attractive to Max. "Oh, there probably is," he responded. "What would you suggest for a *gringo* on his first full day in Cabrito?"

"First off, we need to get you some *libras.* If you go waving dollars around all the time, you are asking to get taken advantage of. I can take you to where you will get the best rate, if you would like."

"Lead on!" replied Max, feeling some of his accustomed self assurance return.

In a small hovel in the poorest section of the most run-down neighborhood in Santo Expedito - called, ironically, *Paraiso* - the mugger known as Cascavel sat and brooded. Until last night his reign of terror had been unbroken in the middle-class *Operários* neighborhood. But this... this *turista* had the nerve to take him on his own turf!

What he needed now was for something to go according to plan. He needed to rob someone else, the way he did every day, and he needed it to go off without a hitch. His confidence had taken a hit, and he needed to build it back up.

With a grim resolve, the wiry street criminal shoved his knife into his waistband and ducked out of the low door of his hut. Straightening up, he squinted until his eyes became accustomed to the bright sunlight. Then, with his face set in a determined scowl, he set off in the direction of *Operários*.

CHAPTER 6

BLACK MOON

*D*iego de Castro was, by all appearances, a man not given to passions. He lived simply, ate sparsely, and his wardrobe consisted of little more than his military dungarees. There was, however, one overwhelming desire that consumed him from the moment the sun rose until long after it had set: Diego craved power.

His method for procuring power had always been to curry favor with those who had it. He did this by making himself useful to them. At first he assumed that the *presidente* was the man in power, and, being in the army, it was relatively easy to get himself stationed to the presidential detail, and then to get noticed by, and become useful to, the chief executive. But it did not take him long to discover that the real power lay not with the current occupant of the *casa branca*, but rather with the Santana family, and more specifically with its favored son: Dr. Emídio Santana.

Dr. Santana was a constant presence at the *casa branca*, much to the obvious irritation of the *presidente*. Diego won favor with

Santana by sharing information, mostly concerning the goings-on at the *casa branca*. An appreciative Santana saw to it that Diego was put on the *gringo*-watch assignment.

Diego had no idea why it was so important that these missionaries be kept out of the country, but he had the feeling that something big was afoot. Whatever the case, it was providing him with plenty of opportunities to be useful to Dr. Santana, and this was a good thing.

After receiving his orders that morning, he busied himself with preparations. The small military truck that had been made available for the "project" was now at the barracks, and Diego had just placed the box of "tools" in the back. He opened it up and examined the contents one more time. When working for Santana, one could not be too careful.

Matches, torches, fuel… it was all there. Now the only thing to do was wait until the set time. Diego's thin lips curved in a satisfied smile as he closed the box. Tonight he would perform yet another valuable service to those in power, and shift one step closer to power himself.

James Madison Rockwell marveled at his good fortune.
Admittedly, he had not been very enthused when his employer, the multinational pharmaceutical conglomerate known as SPGI, had decided that he would oversee the construction of the new factory in Cabrito. The small, virtually unknown island had never been on his list of places to visit before he died.

Yet now that he was here, he found that he did not mind it so much. His trip - in a private jet provided by the grateful government of Cabrito - had been the very definition of comfort - opulent, even. He had been met at the airport by their contact, an international businessman named Santana who spoke impeccable

English. Santana's limo had pulled right onto the tarmac, and then whisked them to the Palácio Hotel, which Santana insisted provided the most luxurious accommodations on the island.

Rockwell believed it. The ten-story building was ancient, but the service was among the best he had received anywhere. As evidence of this, he was at this moment lying facedown on a table, his semi-naked body slathered with some exotic oil. A pretty masseuse named Conchita was gently exorcising aches and pains that, up until then, he had not known existed.

I could really get used to this assignment, he thought.

"Sir? Telephone." Rockwell was about to look up at Conchita when he felt the receiver pressed into his palm. *Now this is service!*

"Hello?"

"Mr. Rockwell," the voice at the other end sounded official. "You are invited to a gala at the presidential residence in celebration of the agreement between SPGI and the nation of Cabrito. A limo will be at the hotel at seven to pick you up."

Well, how do you like that? he thought again. This is going to be the best assignment ever!

Max, also, could not remember having a more enjoyable day. After helping him exchange dollars for *libras*, the lovely creature called Ilana took him on a walking tour of the capital city. They saw picturesque parks, out-of-the-way markets, and the beautiful *Praia Bonita* beach. While traipsing barefoot in the sand beside Ilana, carefully avoiding well-oiled tourists and eager vendors, Max looked out at the ocean. He could make out the lines of what appeared to be a large luxury yacht close to the horizon. Ilana followed his gaze.

"That's the *Lua Negra* - the Black Moon," she explained. "It belongs to the Santana family."

"That's the second time in as many days I have heard that name," Max observed. "I guess they're kind of a big deal around here."

Ilana laughed. "That's putting it mildly. They are what we call in Portuguese the *manda chuvas* - it means 'the ones who send the rain.'"

"And from the looks of that ship, they live it up," Max said, his eyes taking in smooth lines of the yacht. Was that a helicopter he saw sitting on the deck?

"They have a palatial mansion on the ridge overlooking the city, but they almost never use it. George Santana seldom comes here, and his son Emídio pretty much lives on the *Lua Negra.*"

Max turned his attention away from the *Lua Negra.* For some reason the sleek, black craft was making him uncomfortable. It wasn't the yacht itself. No, it was more the impression that they were being watched. He turned to Ilana.

"Luxury yachts, eh? Once you've seen one, you've seen 'em all."

Again Ilana laughed. She thought Max was joking, and he decided to let her think that.

In every man dwells a little Napoleon: a desire to conquer, build, and rule an empire. In men of modest means, this desire manifests itself in stamp collections or model railroads. More ambitious men buy restaurant franchises or build info-tech businesses from scratch.

Men like George Santana are modern-day Napoleons, conquering the world through financial acumen and back-door dealings.

And for me, reflected his son Emídio, *there is Cabrito.*

Emídio was standing on the deck of the *Lua Negra.* In his hands were a pair of high-powered binoculars. He lifted them to his eyes and scanned the island, starting at the tip of the *Dedo de Deus*, and descending slowly until the skyline of Santo Expedito appeared in the foreground. With pleasure, he noted the individual landmarks and reflected on the influence that he had at each one. The binoculars settled on the airport, where a helipad was reserved at all times for his own use, should he deign to grace the island with his presence. His private jet was parked in a nearby hangar. A few blocks to the east was the *Paladar Dourado* restaurant, where he could walk in at any time and get a free meal, waited on hand-and-foot by the entire staff. And if by chance the meat was too rare, or the vegetables overcooked, he could shut the place down with a word.

A couple more blocks over was the Palácio Hotel. There, the top floor was permanently reserved for himself or his special guests. He imagined Mr. Rockwell of SPGI was being treated by Conchita's skillful fingers about now. Santana smiled.

If my American friend knew some of Conchita's other "talents," he might not find his stay so pleasant, he mused.

Scanning a little further east with his binoculars, his eyes came to rest on the *casa branca*. Although he was not its official occupant, Emídio Santana held absolute sway there. His lips curled in satisfied amusement as he recalled yesterday's conversation with the *presidente*.

What a stooge!

A sea swell lifted the yacht, and Emídio found himself looking at a mass of haphazard dwellings hanging precariously on a steep incline. It was the *Paraíso* slum. On a cliff high above that deplorable neighborhood sat *Chantelle*, the historic home of the Santana family since the seventeenth century, named after the French lover of one of his forebears.

Briefly, Santana allowed childhood memories to creep into his consciousness. The absent father whom he worshiped, the indulgent mother he despised, the devoted nanny he adored...

...and suddenly he was back in those halcyon days, days when he ran, carefree and barefoot, through the city of Santo Expedito. Once again he was sneaking out of the house to run the streets with his friends from *Paraíso*.

Then, without warning, his mind's eye saw her, and the pain was too great for him. He lowered the binoculars, shut his eyes, and shook his head as if to physically expel the memory. When he raised the binoculars once again, he was back to his cool, calculating, ruthless self.

This time his gaze settled on the *Operários* neighborhood. Middle-class workers, all toiling hard to make the island - *his* island - function properly. They lived their insignificant little lives in houses that looked much the same, on cobblestone streets that were almost identical. Everything in *Operários* was neat, organized, and controllable... except for *that*.

Emídio focused in on the building that had caught his attention. In a neighborhood of nondescript stucco houses, this one stood out like a sore thumb. It was made of wood - something rare on Cabrito - and had a steeple. It was different from the rounded facade steeples of the Catholic chapels that dotted the island. Nor did it resemble the ornate spires of the cathedral in the center of the city. Instead, it was a simple, unpretentious spire that pointed straight to heaven, as if drawing one's attention to God.

Malditos protestantes!

The Protestant chapel annoyed Emídio for two main reasons. First, he had no influence over this church. All the Catholic churches on the island were personally funded by the Santana family, and naturally, Emídio had clout with the ecclesiastic authorities. But he got the impression that if he were to walk into the Protestant chapel, he would be just another person... and that idea was abhorrent to him.

Second, the Protestant church was always receiving American missionaries. And missionaries were a royal pain in the backside. They taught of a higher Authority to whom all are accountable - something that Emídio Santana, the absolute authority on Cabrito, could not abide. Perhaps they were overly influenced by their American notion of personal liberty, or perhaps it was their theology that had given birth to this obsession with freedom. Whatever the case, it was toxic teaching for people who so obviously needed someone to control them... someone like Emídio Santana.

Yet if it were just a question of theology, the missionaries would be little more than an irritation. But no, the foreign pests had to go sticking their noses into other people's business - more specifically, into *his* business. And this was intolerable. Emídio and his father had plans... big plans... plans a curious missionary could derail.

Unfortunately, as powerful as he was, he could not simply kick them out. There were international treaties to be observed, and his father's financial wheelings and dealings depended in part on the goodwill of the United States' government. Summarily expelling American missionaries could have a negative effect on that.

But there were other ways...

Emídio Santana continued to scan the island. Truth be told, this was one of his favorite pastimes. Cabrito was his personal playground, his very own Garden of Eden. Here he could do anything he wanted and have anything he desired.

And at that moment, he saw something he desired.

His binoculars had found the *Praia Bonita* beach and focused in on a bronze-skinned beauty in a white sundress and matching hat. The man with her, probably some inconsequential tourist here to spend his dollars and make memories, was of no interest. But the girl... he *knew* her!

This was the girl he had sent to the US to study cultural anthropology.

What's her name... Yvonne? Isolde? Ilana! That's it!

She had been little more than a girl when she left. Now... well, obviously her time abroad had been well spent.

Suddenly Emídio was much more enthused about tonight's gala. Of course, he would never let President Ferraz know that. And unfortunately, he would be accompanied by Francesca... but the technicality of matrimony had never stopped him before.

He let his eyes linger on the woman on the beach as she skipped barefoot through the waves that lapped up on the shore. Finally, the man with her took her arm, and they walked back toward the city. Was it his imagination or did the man look straight at him before leading Ilana way?

Santana lowered the binoculars and motioned to an orderly standing discreetly a few feet away.

"Get my clothes ready, and have the mechanic make sure the helicopter is fueled and ready to go. I will be attending a gala at the *casa branca* this evening."

CHAPTER 7

THE SNAKE STRIKES AGAIN

Two o'clock in the afternoon found Ilana and Max eating a late lunch at a small sidewalk café.

"Ilana, you are the best tour guide anybody could ask for," Max said.

"Why, thank you. I'll have to put that on my resumé."

Max chuckled. Though he had been initially awkward, Ilana had put him entirely at ease. Every minute he was with her, he found her to be more delightful. He simply *had* to know more about her. "So, Ilana, tell me about yourself. Are you from Cabrito? What do you do all day - other than rescuing the occasional *gringo* in distress?"

"Oh, I'm from here," she replied. "I was born in an Indian village in the Ipuna jungle, north of here. My mother is a Yamani Indian, and that is where I was raised."

"And your father?" Max asked, and immediately regretted it. Ilana's eyes clouded for the first time since they had met that morning.

"I've never met him. Apparently he was a foreigner who came to our tribe to work on some government project, and I was conceived. When I was a little girl, some people came to the village and said that my father had arranged for me to study at a boarding school here in Santo Expedito. So from that point on, I lived here, going back to the village for vacations. I thought maybe he would come and see me, but he never did."

"Wow," was all Max could think of to say. What could motivate a father to not want to know his daughter - especially one as delightful as this? There was a silence for a few moments as Ilana looked off into the distance. Finally, she continued.

"As to what I do now... after high school I got a scholarship to study in the US. I spent six years at UCLA, getting my Master's in Cultural Anthropology, but I always planned on coming back here to help improve the lot of the Yamani Indians - my people."

"And so you came back."

"Yes. I have just been appointed chief of FUNAPI, the government agency in charge of Indian affairs. In fact, there is a big banquet tonight and... hey!"

"What is it?" Max asked.

"The banquet! I have a banquet at the White House tonight!"

"In Washington?"

"No, silly. Everybody calls the presidential mansion here the White House. It *is* a house, after all, and it's white. Anyway, the invitation said I could bring a guest." She looked at Max. "Would you be my guest at the White House this evening?"

Max chuckled. "When I got up this morning, I never expected to be hearing those words in the afternoon."

"Does that mean yes?"

"Of course. It would be my honor."

Ilana's eyes gleamed. "This is going to be fun! You might even get to meet the president!"

Max had been to his share of formal banquets, and he generally hated them. In fact, his intense distaste for that whole scene had been one of the reasons for the momentous decision during college that had irreversibly changed his life. Normally for Maxwell Sherman, going to a gala banquet would have ranked up there with getting a root canal. And as for meeting the president, well, he had come in contact with more than one tin-pan leader of a third-world country, and the experiences had seldom been pleasant. But as he gazed at the girl across from him, he realized that if she asked him to, he would attend a masquerade ball and sip tea with Mussolini.

"So," he asked, "What is it exactly that you do at this… FUNA-PI?"

"FUNAPI is an acronym for the *National Foundation for the Protection of the Indian*. We are a government agency, but we get heavy funding from a wealthy benefactor."

"That wouldn't happen to be our friend who lives on the yacht, would it?" asked Max innocently.

"Say what you want about him, Dr. Santana has always been very interested in Indian causes. In fact, FUNAPI was his idea. He modeled it after a similar organization in Brazil. And since then he has been very generous in his donations," Ilana defended.

"Fair enough," replied Max. "So what is it you do?"

"Our aim is to preserve the tribal culture from the encroachments of Western civilization. The Yamani Indians live in a pristine tribal society, and we mean to preserve that as much as possible."

Max was interested. "You mean no contact with Westerners whatsoever?"

"Pretty much," replied Ilana.

"Isn't that like… like…" Max struggled for words. "Like consigning a whole people group to the Stone Age?" he finished weakly.

Ilana bristled. "Contact with 'civilization' is always detrimental to these primitive people," she insisted.

"Like in your case?" Max could see from her expression that he had hit a sore spot. "I'm sorry, Ilana. Here you are courteous enough to show me around, and I start debating. Forgive me."

She gave him a fake pout that almost melted him. "Oh, I guess. Come on, we have a gala to get ready for."

Cascavel stood flat against the wall at the street corner and listened to the female voice chatting gaily as it approached. He had his target. Women were easily excitable. Weak. And this one was conversing in what sounded like English. Even better: a tourist. Had Cascavel been a military strategist, he would have called this a "soft target." As he was *not* a military strategist, he simply gripped his knife and waited. The voice got closer and closer, and then…

"Give me all… *aiiiiii!*"

The last sound was an expression of utter disbelief mixed with terror, for when Cascavel jumped out from his hiding place he found himself face-to-face, not with some *turista* girl, but with the very *gringo* who had humiliated him the night before. There was a girl with him, but she was no *turista* either. Cascavel froze. The girls eyes were wide - more with surprise than anything else. The *gringo* had that same exasperatingly quizzical expression that had been on his face during their last encounter.

"Hey, *amigo!*" Max said. "When we met before, I didn't get your name."

"You know this man?" Ilana hissed at him.

"Oh, we had a little misunderstanding last night. I thought we had it all ironed out, though."

Ilana looked at her companion as if seeing him for the first time.

Meanwhile, the *bandido* heard the word "name" and saw a chance to strike some fear into his victims' hearts. "My name is Cascavel!" he exclaimed, making an effort to sound menacing. It failed.

"Cascavel? Hmmmm…" Max fished around in his head for the meaning…Rattlesnake?

"Very good." said Ilana. "Where did you learn Portuguese?"

"Crash course." replied Max.

Cascavel was incredulous. His intended victims were *ignoring him*. Then Max turned in his direction and spoke in Portuguese.

"Would you mind telling us what it is you want?"

"*Me passa a grana.*" Then, so as to avoid all misunderstanding, "Give me all money!"

If Cascavel had been thinking rationally, he would have turned and run, right then. But the humiliation of the previous night, combined with his rage at the way things were going at that moment, prohibited all rational thought. In a blind fury, he lunged at Max.

The American stepped to one side, putting himself between Snake and Ilana. The unexpected movement forced the attacker to change directions. He became unbalanced, and once again found himself lying on the ground, *sans* knife. He looked up to see it gleaming in Max's hand.

"You know, I think I'm going to keep this. It's way too dangerous for you to be playing with on the street."

The casual attitude of the *americano* made Cascavel burn white hot with rage. His hand closed slowly over a shard of glass lying on the ground nearby - what was left of a discarded beer bottle. As Max continued to examine the knife, Cascavel jumped up and in one catlike move had his arm around Ilana's neck, the shard of glass pressed ominously against her throat.

"Give me money, or she die."

Max went cold. It was his fault, he knew. He had let down his guard. But this was no time for self-recrimination; he could bemoan his carelessness later. Right now, every fiber of his body was focused on the present situation, every sense alert. He had been trained for this kind of situation, and his training had been thorough.

"Take it easy there, Snake…"

Suddenly, Snake let out a cry of pain. His hand opened, and the piece of glass fell to the ground. Then the *bandido* felt himself lifted into the air as effortlessly as if he had been a feather. He stayed there for a split second, then came crashing to the ground, flat on his back, the wind momentarily knocked out of him.

Max stared at Ilana, who stood next to Cascavel, legs spread, chest heaving, and still holding the bandit's arm at an angle that could be described as uncomfortable at best.

"You, young lady, are full of surprises," Max said.

She smiled. "The jungle is a good teacher."

"That it is," he replied. "Can you translate something into Kryollo for me to our friend here?"

"Of course." She leaned down and said something to the man. He responded defiantly, and she gave his arm a little twist. He became silent. "Go ahead, Max."

Max leaned over and looked at Cascavel. "Snake, you seem like a decent fellow." Ilana, somewhat surprised, translated. Snake continued to look at him with defiance. Max continued, "I don't know why you find it necessary to mug people. But I just want you to know that I don't have any hard feelings, and that, after you have cooled down a little, I would like to know if there is any way I can help. Okay, let him go, Ilana."

Ilana could not resist a little extra twist of his arm before finally releasing him. Snake got slowly up, dusted himself off, then turned and ran, disappearing down an alley.

Ilana looked at him curiously. "I guess I'm not the only one full of surprises."

Max smiled. "What do you say we call a cab?"

"Sounds good," said Ilana. "I've had enough adventure for one day. There should be a pay phone nearby."

Max opened his wallet and pulled out the business card Ray had given him.

I've already had one brush with death today, he thought as he contemplated the possibility of a precarious ride in the yellow cab. *Why not make it two?*

CHAPTER 8

A NIGHT OF SURPRISES

If Max had been impressed by Ilana's beauty in the market that morning, he was in no way prepared for what he saw when the chauffeur opened the limo door for him that evening. The innocent tropical beauty of this morning had been replaced by a stunning vision of elegance in a black evening gown. An intoxicating perfume filled the air.

"Have I died and gone to heaven?" he asked, when his mouth finally decided to work.

"No," she replied, obviously pleased by his reaction. "It's just me, the little Indian girl from the jungles of Cabrito." That made Max chuckle.

"I guess you can take the girl out of the jungle, but you can't take the jungle out of the girl."

"Careful," she replied, "or I will do to you what I did to the Snake."

Max smiled at the memory. *And I would probably find it quite enjoyable*, he thought.

Had it not been for his companion, Max would most likely have become depressed at the opulence he saw as the car entered the presidential complex. The fountains, the marble, the gold… it all brought back memories, most of them unpleasant.

"Here we go again," he muttered to himself.

"What was that?" asked Ilana.

"Oh, nothing. Just remembered some things I would rather forget."

"*Mister* Max, you are certainly a man of mystery. Someday you must tell me all about *your* past."

Max loathed talking about his past, but he knew that one look into those deep black eyes, mixed with a whiff of whatever perfume it was that she was wearing, would make him sing like a canary. He was certain that if the US Army knew about her, they would completely rewrite the field manual for interrogation.

The limo stopped at the curb. The chauffeur walked around and opened the door. Max stepped out, then extended his hand to Ilana. Together they stood on the patio and got the shock of their lives - each for different reasons.

Over the arched doorway to the reception area was a large sign: *The President and People of Cabrito Welcome SPGI*. Before either of them could say a thing, a short, worried-looking man walked up to them. Ilana spoke.

"Borges, what is the meaning of this?" she asked in Portuguese.

"There has been a… ah… change in plans, senhorita," explained the rotund little man, furiously dabbing at the beads of sweat that gathered on his prominent forehead despite the coolness of the evening. "Because of a scheduling conflict, the banquet in your honor is being combined with a banquet in honor of the arrival of SPGI in Cabrito."

"So instead of celebrating the indigenous peoples of Cabrito, we are celebrating globalization and the arrival of yet another multinational corporation. Is that it?"

"*Senhorita* Ilana, please try to understand. We had to do this, but we did not want to cancel your event either. Trust me, a good portion of the evening is dedicated to a celebration of the savages... er..." Borges saw fire leap into Ilana's eyes at the use of this word. "...natives," he finished weakly.

Ilana sighed and turned to explain the situation to Max. She found him staring at the sign. He looked a little pale.

"Are you okay, Max?"

Max shook his head to clear it. "Fine," he said. He indicated the banner. "I take it plans have changed?"

Ilana explained the situation to him, and he nodded. He could tell she was disappointed, and he determined to cheer her up. Perhaps it would help him put his own thoughts behind him as well. "Well, it's still a ball, and I am still here with the prettiest girl on the island." He gave his companion a crooked smile. "So why don't we go in and have a good time?"

The smile that lit up her face made the effort worth it. "Come on!" she enthused. "I will introduce you to the movers and shakers of the *Republica Cabritana*."

As they walked through the gates, Max cast a quick glance back at the banner. *What are the odds?*

Far away from the lights and music of the gala, Cascavel sat in front of the Igreja da Paz, "Peace Church." He had come there with the purpose of doing some sort of violence: throwing a rock through a window, chipping away at the wooden walls, breaking down the door... something. He had made the connection between this *gringo* and the church, and he figured that if he could not get the man, he would take out his anger and frustration on the church building.

Yet when he arrived at the building, he hesitated. Had not the *gringo* given him ten dollars? Had he not spared Cascavel's life twice when he could have very easily killed him? And had not what had happened to him been his own fault - especially when he was going to attack a woman, like a coward.

Coward! That's what he was. So cowardly that he could not even bring himself to vandalize a church. With a snarl, he raised up the crowbar in his hand, and that was when he heard the engine.

A car! He couldn't be seen doing this. He did not want to spend any more time in prison. *That* was hell on earth.

He dropped the crowbar and dived for the shadows. When the car pulled up, he caught his breath. It was a van, an *army* van!

A man in an olive-green military uniform and DeGaul-style hat got out and went around to the back of the vehicle. Cascavel was almost certain he recognized him as one of the guards from his time in behind bars. The man opened the back doors and pulled out a large crate. He hefted it over to the building and set it down in front of the door, then he opened it and took the various items out, setting them on the sidewalk.

Cascavel caught his breath. It was *him* - a guard so cruel that even his fellow guards called him *O Diabo*, "the devil."

The soldier took a step, and stubbed his toe on the crowbar Cascavel had carelessly left behind in his hurry to get out of sight. *O Diabo* looked at it, then looked around him carefully; his snake-like eyes, unblinking, appeared to glow in the darkness.

Apparently satisfied that there was nobody there, the man bent down again and began removing the contents of the box. To Cascavel, hidden in the shadows, it was obvious what the plan was. *O Diabo* was going to burn down the church.

Cascavel had the overwhelming urge to get out of there. As silently as possible, he began to inch his way down the street. Finally, sure that he was far enough away, he turned to run. Before he could take a step, there was a sickening click behind him, followed by a voice he had hoped he would never hear again.

"Halt, or I will blow your brains out."

His heart at the bottom of his feet, Cascavel slowly raised his hands into the air.

"Turn around."

Cascavel obeyed, and the soldier came closer to get a better look, all the while keeping his revolver pointed straight at the *bandido*'s head.

"Well, well, well. If it isn't my old friend, Cascavel." Diego noticed the *bandido*'s hands were trembling. A sneer curled at his lips. "Oh, you are afraid! You should be. You see, I am no longer a lowly prison guard. I am now a powerful special agent of the *presidente*. And I am about to make your life *very* miserable."

CHAPTER 9

THE MISSIONARY WALTZ

The formalities of the banquet were over, and the lights were turned down. The band was playing *Blue Danube*, and couples were making their way to the dance floor. Ilana looked expectantly at Max. He knew the look, had seen it many times before. She was waiting for him to ask her to dance.

For Ilana, he thought, and smiled at her. *Forgive me, Mary Sue.* "Would you do me the honor?"

"I would be delighted."

And with that, they moved out onto the floor.

"So what did you think of the ceremony?" Ilana asked, once they had settled into the waltz pattern.

With Ilana this close, Max had to work doubly hard to concentrate on what she was saying. "The music was great, the food was outstanding..." Of course neither of those were what she wanted to hear. "I thought you were brilliant, Ilana."

She blushed, obviously pleased with his assessment.

"And the native dance troupe...were those the 'movers and shakers' you were telling me about?"

"First of all," responded Ilana, pretending to scold, "the word is 'indigenous,' not 'native.' Remember whom you are talking to."

"My humblest apologies to the director of FUNAPI," replied Max with a smile.

"Second, the only thing 'native' about them was the feathers... and I have my doubts about those."

"So that is why you made that dig about people who say nice things about the Indians without really knowing the Indians?"

"Yes," replied Ilana. "It is also why I invited the president, Dr. Santana, and the company representative to visit an Indian village for the annual tribal festival."

"Very clever," said Max admiringly. "Public invitation, no way for them to gracefully refuse."

"We Yasmani are primitive, not stupid," Ilana responded coyly. "It will be an amazing experience, something they will never forget. All the tribespeople from all the villages gather together once a year for a week of music, dancing, and games. It will be a good chance for our national leaders to see the best that our culture has to offer."

The waltzed a while in silence, then Ilana looked up at Max.

"How do you think the SPGI rep will handle being in the jungle surrounded by screaming Yamani?" she asked.

"Who, James? I'm sure he'll take it all in stride." As soon as the words left his mouth, he regretted them.

"James? You mean Mr. Rockwell?" Ilana almost stopped dancing.

"Yeah, him. So, are the Yamani really going to be screaming?"

"Oh we make a lot of noise!" To Max's immense relief Ilana didn't purse the question of why he was on a first-name basis with the representative from a multinational pharmaceutical corporation.

"Sounds fascinating!" said Max. "Too bad I am leaving on Monday."

Ilana gave him that fake pout again. "Perhaps I can have them declare it a national holiday so we can ground all flights until then."

Max laughed and swung her around as the music picked up pace. He had not enjoyed ballroom dancing this much since… well… truth be told, he had *never* enjoyed ballroom dancing this much.

Back at the head table, Osvaldo Ferraz was satisfied. He was at the center, in a spot befitting the *presidente*. In case there was any doubt, a plaque in front of his place setting read *"Presidente."* Dr. Santana was relegated to a place on his right, and this made Ferraz happy. On his left was *dona* Julieta, the first lady. Beside her was Mr. Rockwell of the SPGI. Santana was sitting next to *dona* Francesca, his Brazilian supermodel trophy wife. She looked like she would rather be anywhere else.

In fact, mused the *presidente* to himself, *she always looks that way when she's with Dr. Santana. Poor thing.*

Dr. Santana had met his wife while on a business trip in Rio. Word had it that she had been charmed by Santana's charisma, and his money. Their courtship had lasted just long enough for Santana to divorce his previous wife. From the looks of things, a happy marriage depended on something other than charisma and money.

Ferraz's eyes strayed over to the new FUNAPI director as she danced with her escort. She was clearly the most beautiful woman in the room. *Even Francesca must realize that,* he thought. *That may be contributing to her displeasure as well.*

So far the evening had gone according to plan, even though that plan had been changed only the day before. Ilana's impromptu invitation during her speech was quite unexpected, but Dr. Santana had made no outward sign of displeasure.

The fact was, Dr. Santana was very pleased at the invitation, because it would give him a chance to spend some time with the lovely Ilana, sans Francesca, and sans whoever this annoying American moving her deftly around the dance floor was. From his seat at the head table, the scion of Cabrito's ruling family could not keep his eyes off the lovely apparition dancing in the middle of the ballroom, despite the cold stare he felt from his wife.

My how she has blossomed! Santana watched Ilana move gracefully across the floor. *She is even more beautiful now than when I saw her on the beach this morning! Last I knew, she was a gangly teenager I was putting through boarding school and college. Now...* que mulher!

Emídio Santana was accustomed since childhood to getting whatever he desired. Right now, he desired Ilana. His mind began to formulate the plan that would put her in his arms. The fact that he was married to a beautiful woman - the one sitting right next to him - did not even figure into his calculations.

His reverie was interrupted by a tap on the shoulder. He turned to see Diego standing respectfully in the background. The *presidente* turned at the same time.

"Diego," said Ferraz. "We have been waiting for you."

"Yes, *senhor presidente*," responded Diego.

"You bring news?" It was Dr. Santana this time.

"Yes, sir. I regret to inform you that a terrible tragedy has befallen the church of the *protestantes*, and it has burned to the ground. In an interesting further development, a marginal element was apprehended at the spot, and he will most likely be charged with the crime."

"Splendid!" said both the *presidente* and Dr. Santana at once. "Well done, soldier," added Dr. Santana.

"Thank you, sir. I..." Diego stopped and stared at the dance floor.

"What is it?" asked Ferraz. "What's the matter, Diego?"

The military man pointed. "That man, dancing with Ilana."

"Yes, that is her escort for the evening," said Ferraz. "Some American tourist. I met him. Maxwell something-or-other."

"He is no tourist," Diego hissed. "It's *him* - the *missionário* that you want me to get rid of!"

"Missionaries dance?" President Ferraz asked, incredulously.

"This one does, and quite well, apparently," Diego replied.

In his infatuation with Ilana, Dr. Santana had all but ignored her her dancing partner. Now an ardent jealousy burned in his heart. Maintaining his outward calm, he looked at the *presidente* and raised an eyebrow. "We want this man out of the country, and yet here he is, in the presidential mansion, cheek-to-cheek with the new FUNAPI director? Rather odd, don't you think?"

"Well... I..." Ferraz was totally unprepared for this. "You know what they say. Keep your friends close, keep your enemies closer..." he finished weakly.

"Yes, this explains why you have me seated right next to you," observed Dr. Santana icily. "It would seem I have some planning to do." He stood up.

"*Senhor Presidente, dona* Julieta. Come, Francesca. We must leave now."

Francesca made no attempt to hide the scorn on her pretty face as she stood. Dr. Santana turned to Diego.

"Come, Diego."

Diego beamed and followed the *doutor* and *dona* Santana out.

Presidente Osvaldo Ferraz put his head in his hands. It had been going so well. Now he was going to have to do some serious damage control. His mind was suddenly racked with fears about what Santana's "planning" might involve.

So engrossed was Ferraz in his own problems that he did not notice how James Madison Rockwell, official representative of the SPGI conglomerate, was staring intently at the man dancing with Ilana.

This assignment just got a lot more interesting, Rockwell mused. In his hand he fingered a piece of paper that Francesca Santana had surreptitiously dropped on his plate as she passed behind him. He began to look for a way to graciously exit the proceedings.

Ray sat at the bar in the *Macaco Verde*. A full mug of beer sat in front of him. It was his second of the night, and at the rate he was going, it would be empty before long. His mind was troubled, and long years of conditioning had taught him that the cure for a troubled mind was an alcoholic beverage.

It usually worked, too - at least for a little while. Today, however, the alcohol was running off his conscience like water poured on a smooth, oil-covered stone. He banged his fist on the bar.

Of all the taxicabs in all the banana republics in all the world…

He had been home when the call came from Max. They were together, Max and *her*. They got into the taxi and chatted gaily the entire time. Up until that point, Ray had not even known that she was back, that she was here in Cabrito. Now he was beginning to suspect that she was a part of something a lot bigger than he had imagined. And this was just the opposite of what he wanted to happen.

Ray, ol' boy, his mind was saying, *you really need to stay sharp to be on top of this situation.* As if to defy his thoughts, he took a long drink, almost emptying the mug. He felt a tap on his shoulder, and someone put a note on the bar in front of him. He opened it, not even bothering to see who had left it.

"A great tragedy has befallen the Protestant church. We expect that Sr. Maxwell will be ready to leave the country at the earliest possible moment. Please be ready to accommodate him."

Diego. Always efficient. Always covering his bases.

Ray spent another few minutes thinking about all the possible implications of the note he had just received. Then he ordered another beer.

CHAPTER 10

FROM THE ASHES

The capricious whimsy of dreams had whisked the slumbering Max back to upstate New York, back to the Greensborough Community Church. The service was just beginning. Pastor Dave was talking to the organist. Max scanned the bulletin. None of the songs were familiar to him. In fact, the bulletin seemed to be written in a different language altogether - Kryollo, if he was not mistaken.

He nudged Mary Sue. "Wonder why they wrote this in Kryollo."

"Why not?" came the answer, but it wasn't Mary Sue's voice. Max turned and nearly jumped out of his skin. Sitting beside him was a smiling Ilana!

"What are you doing here?" Max asked, half rising. Ilana didn't answer him - she just kept smiling.

"That is what I would like to know!" Now *that* was Mary Sue's voice. Max turned to see his girlfriend standing in the aisle, her hands on her hips, a look of extreme displeasure on her pretty face. "Who is this woman?"

"Um, Mary Sue, this is… um…" His voice trailed off. Somewhere in the distance the church organ began to play *Blue Danube*.

"Max, could you come here and help me, please?" It was Pastor Dave. Max, relieved to have an excuse to extract himself from the awkward situation, stood and tried to slide past Mary Sue.

"Max, you are not going anywhere." Mary Sue stood firm.

"Max?" It was Ilana. Max turned to see that she had a Bible open on her lap. "Max, there is a lot here I don't understand. Can you explain it to me?"

"Max!" Mary Sue again. "Why is this woman talking to you?"

"Max." It was Pastor Dave. "Max, I really need your help up here."

"Max." It was a new voice behind him. Max turned to see Mr. Blake in the pew behind him, his family sitting there with him. "Max, take my advice and get out of Cabrito while you can."

"Max!"

"Max!"

"Max!"

"Aaaaaah!" Max sat up in his bed, sweat pouring from his body. His heart raced, and he took deep breaths to calm himself.

"Max!"

That voice was real, and it came from outside the house. It was accompanied by several short raps on the door.

"*Missionário* Max! Come quick!"

Now Max recognized the voice. It was Isabela. He jumped out of bed and headed out of the house, pulling on a shirt as he went. When he opened the gate, he found Isabela with her father and a couple other men he did not know.

"*Missionário* Max, please hurry. The church is burning!"

Now completely awake, Max could see the glow of the fire in the distance. He closed the door behind him and followed the men and Isabela. As they drew closer to the blaze, the air became thick with smoke. They turned the corner, and Max instinctively put his arms up to ward off the intense heat.

The church building was a blazing inferno. Flames reached into the sky and shot sparks at the stars. The entire neighborhood was in the street. The women and children watched the fire while the men filled buckets with water. Max saw that they were not even trying to put out the fire. Rather, they were watching to see where the sparks fell and rushing to put them out so the fire would not spread.

"Where's the fire department?" Max asked. Isabela pointed to a pickup parked in the shadows. Three men in uniform stood around, haphazardly directing the efforts of the men with buckets.

Helpless to do anything, Max stood with the others and watched as the fire slowly burned itself out. The timbers fell, one by one, into glowing heaps, and the roaring blaze turned into a warm glow. The families returned to their homes, mothers and children first, then the fathers. Convinced that all danger was past, the firemen piled into their pickup and drove off, leaving only Max and the other members of the church standing around to observe the damage.

Max had only seen the church building in pictures. Now he was seeing it for the first time - as an ash heap. As the first glow of dawn crept up on Max, he felt the despair and sadness of the people around him. He did not know them, but they were his brothers and sisters in Christ. And he felt, profoundly, their loss.

As their eyes welled up with tears, so did his. He had heard Bernardinho talk with pride about how the families had sacrificed their own finances to add to offerings from churches in the US, and then erected the building with their own hands.

Now it was a smoldering ruin.

Suddenly the shrill whine of a siren broke the mood. A military van pulled up, and a soldier in an olive-green uniform got out. He addressed the group in Kryollo. Max looked to Isabela for a translation.

"He say that a bad man started the fire last night. They catch him. He is in prison now."

Hearing the words in English, the soldier turned his attention to Max. His yellow, snakelike eyes sized Max up. Max noticed the name patch on his chest. *Diego*. He looked vaguely familiar, but the American could not place him. Diego walked up to him.

"You American, yes?" He surveyed the wreckage of the church building. "Such a shame. I think maybe this happen because of you. The man we catch… he say he have fight with you. His name is Cascavel…Rattlesnake."

At the mention of that name, Max's mind went to high alert. He did not at all like the way this soldier was singling him out. *Snake? Responsible for this?* Max had his doubts. Still, they *had* had a run-in--two to be exact.

Diego continued. "Better if you leave Cabrito. Very dangerous here. Things can happen… bad things…*very* bad things." Abruptly, he turned and spoke something in Kryollo, so the little congregation could hear. Then he turned, got in the truck, and drove off.

"He say that when there is American involved, there is always trouble," whispered Isabela.

Max's blood ran cold. He knew a threat when he heard one, and this was most certainly a threat. Whether they came from his mother, his employer, enemy combatants, or girlfriends, threats always had a reverse effect on him. While many people chose to run when threatened, it was in Max's nature to dig in and fight.

What would Adoniram Judson do? Max asked himself. He looked at the devastated members of the congregation. They were saddened, frightened, confused, and leaderless.

Leaderless people attract leaders like a vacuum. Max began speaking to the people in low tones, consoling them as best his command of the Portuguese would allow.

"What are we going to do now?" one of the *senhoras* asked him. Everybody looked at him, awaiting his answer. Max thought for a moment then spoke slowly.

"One of the first lessons I learned after I became a believer in Christ is that a church is not a building." His mind went back to his first week as a new convert, when Pastor Dave had explained these things to him. "Whoever did this destroyed a building, but they will never be able to destroy the church. So you just need to go about doing the things you have always done…just without a building.

There was a general assent in the small crowd as Max's words were translated. He continued, "Why doesn't everybody come to my… er… the Blakes' house tonight. We can have a service there."

As he spoke, he could see skepticism and fear in people's eyes. Diego's statement had obviously taken its effect. Bernardinho began talking to the small congregation, encouraging them to be at the former Blake residence that evening.

While the people conversed amongst themselves, Max turned around to look at the smoldering wreckage of the church building. His experienced eyes scanned the scene. Point of combustion, accelerant...arson.

He shook his head as memories of other burned-out buildings from another life flashed through his brain.

Snake? Not likely. The erstwhile mugger may have had motive, but he was impulsive. The charred rubble before Max screamed planning and execution. Who would do this?

Again Max shook his head and looked down. It was then that he saw the truck tracks. They were very clear in the thin sand that dusted the top of the cobblestone pavement. Following the tracks with his eye, Max was able to picture the vehicle as it pulled up to the front of the church, stopped, and then pulled away. How old were they? A day? By their condition it could not have been more than a day - or early last night. Then he looked at the fresher tracks made by the military vehicle that had just left.

They were identical!

Definitely not the Snake, Max mused. He reflected on how the soldier named Diego had "just happened" to show up. He briefly considered sharing his observations with Bernardinho, then thought better of it. Whoever was behind this was capable of great evil, and the less others knew, the safer they were - for the time being.

Max turned around, and saw that most of the congregation had left.

"You must eat lunch with us." It was Isabela, motioning him to accompany her and her family. "My father wants you to eat every meal with us until you leave."

"He might want to re-think that."

"Why?"

Max smiled wryly. "Because I will not be leaving Cabrito anytime soon."

"He will be on the first flight out of Cabrito," said Diego with satisfaction. "Right now he is probably frightened beyond belief. I can be very intimidating."

Dr. Santana appraised the soldier in front of him. Ruthless, efficient, completely devoid of principles: the kind of man that was to be used - but kept at arm's length. He had to admit, however, that so far Diego's work had been impressive. In a single move, he had delivered a strong message to the American intruder, destroyed the Protestant church, and - icing on the cake - provided the pretext to remove another petty criminal from the streets. Not to mention his handling of the American taxi driver. Ray had been a useful stooge for many years, but ever since Diego had become his handler, he had been much more cooperative.

With the American gone, there would be one less barrier to Santana's plans, both for the island of Cabrito and for Ilana. Once again, visions of that divinely beautiful woman filled Santana's mind - something that had been occurring with increasing frequency since the banquet. In his mind's eye, he could see her running toward him - in slow motion, no less - on the beach. When she reached him, she embraced him and began to cover his face with kisses.

"Oh, Dr. Santana!" she murmured.

"Please, call me Emídio."

"Dr. Santana?"

The voice was not Ilana's, but Diego's - interrupting his fantasy. Santana looked at him irritably.

Diego cleared his throat awkwardly and continued. "I can guarantee you that there will be no Protestant church service tonight in Santo Expedito," he said.

It had been a long night for James Madison Rockwell. He had discovered one of the major downsides to living on Cabrito island: the precarious telephone system. Internet was unknown on the island, and using the phone - especially for someone wanting to make an international call - could be very frustrating.

He tried to call numerous times on Saturday night, with no success. Finally, early Sunday morning, he resorted to a satellite phone the company had provided him for use in emergencies. After a couple rings, a woman's voice answered the other line. Mr. Rockwell took a deep breath.

"I am sorry to bother you on a weekend, ma'am, but there is something you should know."

CHAPTER 11

THE ZIKLAG ANALOGY

Cascavel sat in a fetal position in the corner of his dank cell. When he had been released from prison three years ago, he'd sworn he would never go back. Now here he was, being punished for something he didn't do. Or, more accurately, for something he *almost* did. Handcuffed to the back of the car, he had watched Diego - *O Diabo* - burn the Protestant church to ashes.

Now he was in jail, about to be accused of that very crime. He shivered in the miserable cold. *Why?* he cried inwardly. *Why did these things happen to him? Why did his life have to be so hard?*

"Hey, Worm! Get up!" A guard stood at the gate and called him by the nickname he had been given during his previous time in jail. It was a cruel mockery of his street *nom de guer.*

Slowly, Cascavel stood and shuffled to the iron bars that separated him from the guard. At the signal, he stretched out his arms, and the guard snapped cuffs on his wrists. Then the guard put a key in the door, and its rusty hinges groaned at the inconvenience of opening.

Pushing the hapless prisoner before him, the guard wound his way through the dark labyrinth that was the *Prisão Federal*. Cascavel shuddered as he remembered the horrors he had previously endured as a prisoner here.

They moved up a set of stairs, through a better-lit section of the building, and finally to a big, wooden door. The guard opened it, pushed Cascavel through, and then shut it behind him. The hapless bandit took in his surroundings quickly: sparse furnishings, a big desk flanked on each side by flags - the national flag and that of the Cabritan Army.

And there, sitting at the desk, was *o Diabo*. To Cascavel's surprise, *O Diabo* smiled pleasantly at him, then got up from the desk and stepped toward him. Instinctively, Cascavel moved back. *O Diabo* extended his hand, and Cascavel shrank from it. Then he saw that the hand was holding a key. In shock, he watched as *o Diabo* put the key in the handcuffs and turned it clockwise. The cuffs fell away from his hands, and Cascavel stood there, unable to hide his astonishment.

Diego motioned to a wooden chair in front of his desk. "Have a seat, *amigo*."

"*Amigo?*" He asked incredulously. Was this some kind of a joke?

Diego smiled and continued to motion toward the chair. Not having much choice, Cascavel sat. Diego went back around the desk and sat opposite him. He reached into a drawer and produced a long wooden box.

"Cigar?" he offered. "They're Cuban."

"No, thanks," Cascavel mumbled.

"Suit yourself," said Diego as he pulled one out, put it in his mouth, and lit it. "It just seemed like an appropriate way to celebrate our new partnership."

"Come again?" Cascavel was curious, yet wary at the same time. He had suffered too much at the hand of this man in the past to believe what he was hearing now.

"I'm sorry, I guess I owe you an explanation." Diego removed the cigar from his mouth and waved it expressively as he talked. "You see, I think it is a good time for you and I to turn over a new leaf in our relationship. I have been doing a little research on your past, and it seems to me you have a… shall we say, skill set that could be very useful to me."

"What do you mean?"

Diego looked him straight in the eye. "You, sir, are a thief."

Cascavel stood up, enraged at the insult. "Why, you…"

Diego waved him back into the chair with a laugh. "Sorry, my friend. I didn't mean to offend. Actually, I meant it as a compliment."

"What?"

"You see," Diego explained, leaning forward at his desk, "You have quite the reputation. After bringing you here last night, I did a little research. The crimes of which you are suspected - and it *is* an impressive list, I might add - made me take a second look at you. For example…" he rummaged through his papers. "This one here. You stole some jewels from a family that lives in a third-story apartment in the *Operários* neighborhood." He looked at Cascavel, who by his expression was neither confirming or denying.

"Or what about this one?" he continued, holding up an official-looking document. "You stole five thousand dollars' worth of electronic equipment from a delivery truck *while it was being driven*."

Cascavel couldn't help but smile at that recollection. Diego noticed it.

"So it *was* you! I *knew* it!" Seeing Cascavel's flustered expression, he waved his hand again. "Don't worry. Don't you see? This is why I am so interested in you. I am offering you the chance to work for me."

"Work for you?" Cascavel was dumbfounded. How could he work for this man, this *monster* of a man, whom he hated with a passion? Diego read his thoughts.

"Oh, I know we have had our issues in the past. But I think you will agree, working for me will be much better than rotting in jail. Besides, I think you and I have a common enemy."

"Common enemy?"

"Word on the street is that you had a run-in with a certain American *turista*. The people I work for are very anxious for this *gringo* to leave the island. I'm sure you are, too. We're fairly sure he is going on Monday, but we need to be positive. This is where you come in. With your special abilities, you can follow him and keep us up to date as to his movements."

Cascavel's head was swimming. Was he really going to be working *for* the government, and against this annoying *gringo*?

"Give the word," Diego continued, "and we will get you a hot bath, some clean clothes, and a good meal. Or, you can just go back to your cell and wait for justice," he indicated the stack of papers on his desk, "to be served. What do you think?"

Cascavel looked at him, and a smile spread across the thief's face. "I think I'd like to smoke that cigar now... boss."

Max's heart was pounding so fiercely he was sure others could hear it. His hands were clammy, and sweat beaded on his brow. He was not a fearful man. Indeed, in his short lifetime he had faced down dangerous enemies with a quiet calm that had earned him the respect of friend and foe alike. Yet now it was with great difficulty that he suppressed the panic welling up inside him.

Idiot! When they asked you to speak, why didn't you just say "No"?

They were on the front lawn of the former Blake residence. Chairs had been set up on the carefully manicured grass, and the people of Igreja da Paz were seated before him. Bernardinho was standing next to him, giving a somewhat lengthy introduction. Max assumed he was explaining a little background as to the presence of the americano in their midst. It was Sunday evening, and Max was about to deliver his first-ever sermon. Oh sure, he'd led a Bible study back in New York, and even taught the occasional Sunday School class. Pastor Dave, impressed with his quick grasp of biblical subjects had asked him to fill the pulpit once or twice on Sunday evenings, but Max had always found a reason to politely refuse.

Now he had no choice, and it was going to be in Portuguese.

After what seemed like forever, Bernardinho sat down. Max looked at the crowd, gulped, and began.

"I... I really have no idea why I am here."

Excellent start, Max, old boy. Way to instill confidence in your listeners! Max could see some of them shifting uncomfortably in their seats.

"My name is Max, and I came here to help with an addition to the church building. I guess I have my work cut out for me." His attempt at humor fell flat, so he forged ahead.

"It seems to me that everybody is confused, discouraged, and perhaps a little afraid. The truth is, so am I. I have no idea why God brought me here, only to have the missionaries leave and the church burn down. It seems like things are going from bad to worse. I wish I had answers, but I don't.

"Ever since I became, you know, a follower of Jesus, I have liked the Old Testament. I like the stories of battles, of blood and guts, of adventure." Max paused as he noticed his listeners collectively furrow their brows. Apparently "blood and guts" didn't work in Portuguese. Doggedly, he pushed forward.

"One of my favorite people to study is David. He was a warrior, a fighter, and at the same time, he was a man after God's own heart. This afternoon I re-read one of my favorite stories from David's life, a story my pastor pointed out to me when I was going through a discouraging time as a new convert. You can read it in the book of 1 Samuel, chapter thirty."

Max paused while the people found the passage in their Portugueses Bibles, then he read it. His translation of the Bible was written in a stilted, archaic prose, much different from the language he had studied in his crash course. Still, as he struggled through all but abandoned verb tenses, his mind imagined the scene being described: David, leader of a small band of soldiers of fortune, returns from a fight to find Ziklag - the city where they lived - burned to the ground and their wives and children kidnapped.

The men naturally blame their leader, and there is talk of a military execution without benefit of court-martial.

He stopped there and looked up at the assembled believers.

"You see, David was kind of in the same boat we are in."

Once again the furrowed brows. Ok…they weren't in a boat…

"The same situation…"

The brows collectively un-furrowed.

"Everything was going wrong for him. He lost his family and belongings, and his own men were mad at him and wanted to kill him. But David had God's promise that he was going to be king someday, so he did not give up. Instead, he asked God for guidance, and God gave them a victory over their enemies."

Max sensed he had their attention. Encouraged, he continued.

"Now, the way it seems to me, we have some pretty incredible promises too. One of the first verses I memorized as a new Christian was Romans 8:28 - 'all things work together for good, to those who love God, who are called according to His purpose.' Not only that, but all of us know that God loved us so much that he sent Christ, His only Son, to die for us. So we know God is on our side, and we know He has a plan.

"Like I said, I have no idea what that plan is. But I am very curious to find out. When I first got here, and the Blakes left, my only thought was to get off this island as soon as possible. But now… now I want to stay. If you are willing, I want to work alongside you here and see what God will do. That's… that's kind of all I have to say."

With that, he sat down. Slowly Bernardinho got up and began to speak in Kryollo. Max thought he saw tears in his eyes. Isabela leaned over and whispered in his ear.

"He says he is convinced that God sent you for just this time. He is saying that the church should invite you to take the place of the Blakes. Everybody who agrees should stand up."

Max was about to protest when a diminutive old lady sitting next to him stood up. He remembered Bernardinho telling him that she had been the first convert at the Igreja da Paz - a woman who had endured great hardship for her commitment to Christ. The young boy next to her - her grandson - followed suit. Then another, and another, and another until every member of the Igreja da Paz was on their feet.

Bernardinho looked at Max, who was still sitting. Slowly but deliberately, he got to his feet. Somewhere in the back, someone began singing *Amazing Grace* in Portuguese.

> *Oh! graça sublime do Senhor, perdido me achou;*
> *Estando cego, me fez ver, Da morte me salvou.*

Max sang along quietly in English. When the song was over, Bernardinho looked at the young American in front of him. In English, he said, "Welcome, Missionary Max."

Leaning against the wall behind the former Blake residence, Ray could hear nearly everything that went on in the yard. The Bible story Max had told had brought back memories of a long-departed time, of sunny days, a happy family, and a white-clapboard church in the middle of vast midwestern cornfields.

The last part of the service, the impromptu commissioning of a missionary, brought the crusty American expatriate crashing back to reality.

He's going to stay!

Upon reflection, Ray was not all that surprised. When he had first met the boy, he had known there was a quality about him that Diego and company could not see. He carried himself with a quiet, watchful assurance. Ray knew there was only one school that produced such men. He himself was a graduate of the same *alma mater*.

The "powers that be" on the island wanted him gone. And Ray was going to have to cooperate in making sure that happened; forces beyond his control would make sure of that. He would do it, but he wouldn't like it.

It's for her, and for her I would blow up the entire island of Cabrito, Ray thought. His mind turned back to the young American. *This is going to be an interesting contest.*

Slowly, Ray walked back to his taxi, hidden in an alley two blocks away. He was just about to open the beat-up Volkswagen's door when a shiny black sedan turned the corner and gunned past him, roaring down the cobblestones in the direction Ray had just come from. Ray stopped and rubbed his jaw thoughtfully. In the driver's seat, he had clearly seen Ilana.

CHAPTER 12

THE MERCEDES BUG

fter the service ended, people crowded around Max, wanting to know everything about this young man who had spoken so fervently to them, breathing life into their little congregation. They peppered him with questions, and poor Isabela did valiant work in translating them.

Finally, it was over, and he was alone with Bernardinho's family. They set up a meeting for the next day with the deacons of the church and exchanged ideas about where to go from here. After that, Max saw them to the metal door that opened from the courtyard to the road outside. As he let them out, he noticed the shiny black Mercedes parked in front of the house. Leaning on the hood, in jeans and a Lakers T-shirt, was Ilana.

Surprised but pleased to see her, Max introduced her to Bernardinho. When he mentioned that she was the director of FU-NAPI, his eyes grew wide. Bernardinho was a simple man, unaccustomed to contact with the "rich and powerful." After a few awkward pleasantries, he and his family excused themselves and began the trek home, leaving Ilana and Max alone at the gate.

"To what do I owe the pleasure of your company?" asked Max.

"Aren't you going to invite me in?" asked Ilana coyly. Then, seeing Max's reluctance, "I just want to talk."

"Tell you what," replied Max, recovering his poise. "Why don't we find a little establishment that's open this time of night, and we can talk as much as you want."

"Okay!" she said eagerly. "I know just the place."

"Great. And I'm buying."

"Such a gentleman," said Ilana with a giggle. "Shall we take my wheels?" She indicated the car, which Max could now see was a Mercedes.

"Seeing as, between us, you are the only one *with* wheels, that sounds like a good idea. Nice ride, by the way."

"Thanks! It was delivered this morning. A personal expression of gratitude from Dr. Santana himself."

Max shook his head in mock sadness. "Oh, the corrupting influence of civilization on indigenous culture!"

Ilana shot him a withering glance, then got into the driver's seat. Chuckling, Max slipped into the passenger seat.

"This is nice," he said as the leather seats and air conditioning assaulted his senses with levels of comfort he had not felt since leaving the US. He ran his hand admiringly over the vinyl dashboard in front of him, and then stopped cold.

How interesting. As his fingers slipped underneath the dashboard they ran across the wiring that was definitely *not* factory-issue. *This car is bugged!*

The question was, who was bugging it? With his hand still under the dash, he cast a glance at Ilana. She looked at him and gave him a broad smile.

Either she is a very good actress, he thought, *or she knows nothing of this.*

Ilana started the engine. "I am so glad we get one more chance to talk before you go back to the US tomorrow," she said seriously. "I think I'll take you to one of my favorite places - the *Paladar Dourado.*"

Max could not get his mind off the electronic listening device under the dash.

Time to send a message, he decided.

"I'm really glad you stopped by, but I won't be leaving tomorrow after all. In fact, I don't think I'll be going anywhere anytime soon."

"Really!" Ilana was overjoyed. "I'm so glad to hear that! What made you change your mind?"

This was the question Max was hoping for.

"It's all about this little church I came to help." He briefly explained the arson at the church building and his assessment of it - leaving out the visit by the soldier. Ilana was horrified.

"Who do you think is behind it?"

"I have no idea." Max leaned forward, wanting whoever was listening to hear his next words well. "But I *will* find out."

Ilana seemed doubtful. "A lot of things happen on this island that are never explained. Still, if there is any way I can help - being a government official and all..."

"Thanks, but I can be very resourceful." Max decided it was time to change the subject. "So what did you want to talk about so badly that you made a special trip this evening - in your brand-new Mercedes?"

Ilana blushed. "You intrigue me, Max. You come off as a simple, down-to-earth guy, yet at the banquet last night, you seemed perfectly at ease. And the way you danced! Clearly, you are no stranger to high society."

Good thing my mom's not here, Max thought. *She would get no end of satisfaction out of hearing that.*

"You're a puzzle, Max," Ilana went on. "And I like puzzles. Besides, I told you my story the other day. You owe me."

"Fine. I just hope I don't bore you out of your skull."

"I see very little chance of that." Ilana gunned the motor and the Mercedes sped through the vacant, winding streets of Santo Expedito.

Once again, Max found himself hanging on for dear life. Though Ilana's car was a vast improvement over Ray's, her driving was not.

In the corner of a run-down warehouse in *Praia Seca*, Diego adjusted the volume on his headset. This listening post had been his idea, and Dr. Santana had given it his immediate approval. Diego was seated in front of a large black panel. Wires led from it into the ceiling, and from there to antennas fastened to the corrugated metal roof. On the panel, which was actually a large sound board, there were several channels, each one marked with a piece of adhesive tape. Currently Diego's headset was connected to the channel marked "Ilana's Car."

Now Diego sat still, unable - or unwilling - to process what he had just heard. The *americano* was *staying*! This was not welcome news. It meant that his strong-arm tactics had been a failure. The burned-down building, the threats… all for nothing. The *gringo* had not been intimidated. In fact, it appeared as if just the opposite had taken place.

Diego furrowed his brow. He would have to think hard about how to present this unpleasant information to Dr. Santana. Experience told him that Santana did not tolerate failure in others. Lying to him was out of the question. He would find out the truth sooner or later.

One thing was for sure: this unexpected development made it all the more essential that the next phase of the operation went well. He reached for a walkie-talkie on the table and adjusted the frequency. Time to talk to his new associate.

Just then the black phone on the table in front of him rang. He picked up the receiver, fearing he would have to give a report to Santana at that moment. When he heard the voice on the other end, he breathed a sigh of relief. It was Ray.

"Yes, I know the *americano* is staying." Diego paused while the man on the other end spoke. "Well, obviously, *you* are not being very effective in getting him to leave. I suggest you come up with a plan, and quick!" With that, he hung up the phone, then picked up the walkie-talkie again.

Perhaps my new associate will be more motivated for success, he thought as he pressed the "talk" button.

"*Alô*, Cascavel, do you read me?"

On an otherwise-deserted street corner, Ray slammed down the receiver in disgust. Diego was slime, and he cursed the day he had ever gotten mixed up with him. His original agreement had been with Santana himself, and that had been taxing enough. But when Santana delegated his extortion work to the smug, irritating, posturing Diego... Well, things had gotten pretty unbearable from that day forward.

Now events were spinning quickly out of Ray's control. Max had befriended Ilana, Diego had bungled an attempt at intimidation to the point that Max was going to stay, and somehow he, Ray, was going to have to fix it. He also wondered how Diego had known Max was staying before he did.

Shaking his head, he trudged back to the Volkswagen, opened the door, and sat down. He stayed there for a few moments, trying to sort things out. There was only one solution: get Max off the island. It would be better for him, better for Ilana... better for everybody. The only problem was, Max apparently didn't scare easily. With the Blakes, it had been easy - one could always count on maternal instincts to kick in. But with Max there was no wife, no kids.

Threatening Ilana was out of the question, and other than her... wait! There *was* someone Max cared for - perhaps enough to get out of Dodge in order to ensure their safety! With a set jaw and a steely expression, Ray started his car and began the trip home, his mind already formulating a plan.

Santo Expedito at night - when seen from the tenth-floor luxury suite of the Palácio Hotel - is truly breathtaking. Starting at the beach, the city lights spread like a luminescent spider web through the downtown area and continue unabated through the upscale residential district, following the contour of the land as it rises like a giant wave. The lights of the poor districts are more chaotic and begin to dissipate as the mountain continues to rise, until finally all that is left is a thin trail that indicates the presence of a road. This is the main route leading from Santo Expedito to the towns on the other side of the island.

James Madison Rockwell stood on the balcony of his tenth-floor suite and inhaled deeply on his cigarette, blowing the smoke out in one long stream. He leaned on the railing and gazed out at the view before him, yet his mind was far from the aesthetic beauty of nocturnal Santo Expedito. Instead, he was thinking about the telephone call he had just received.

So she is coming here.

He ran his hand over his shiny, bald head as if to suppress any rogue hairs that may have appeared since his last glance in the mirror. Then the cigarette went back into his mouth, and he puffed furiously, his brow furrowed in concentration.

A quarter century. That was how long he had worked for SPGI. James Rockwell's specialty was going into new areas and opening up factories. He loved working out the details of supply, transportation, and labor; he thrilled at the challenge of starting with a vacant lot and leaving a fully functioning, profit-generating facility. He put himself to sleep at night thinking of all the jobs he had created, while at the same time trying to ignore nagging doubts about globalization, domestic unemployment, and exploitation of cheap labor.

The nature of his work also forced him to turn a blind eye to the unsavory aspects of the countries that hosted him. Bribes to corrupt officials, buying land and raw materials at prices that served to line powerful pockets, watching governments strong-arm their own citizens in favor of a multinational corporation - it was all in a day's work for him.

One thing was certain: never, *ever* in all of those twenty-five years had the CEO come to personally oversee his work. Not that he had anything to hide. He was the consummate professional, always sending back thorough and accurate reports. He took great pride in the fact that he had personally contributed to the success of SPGI over the years, and his superiors - including the CEO - had complete and well-placed faith in him.

Yet now, sometime in the near future, he would be receiving a personal visit from *her*. He knew it had nothing to do with his performance. Rather, it was because of the phone call he had made this morning. Yet he also knew that she would expect him to have the situation well under control upon her arrival. It was time to be proactive.

I think I shall have to pay the young Mr. Sherman a visit.

CHAPTER 13

SLIPPERY SLOPE

*C*ascavel placed the walkie-talkie down and looked through the binoculars, scanning the lighted streets below him. He was perched on the tile roof of a two-story residence in downtown Santo Expedito. It was where all the upscale restaurants were, and it was where *Diego* - formerly known as *O Diabo* - had informed him that Max and Ilana would be dining.

As he watched the cars pass on the lighted streets around him, Cascavel reflected on the dramatic change in his relationship with Diego.

And it's all because of this meddlesome American, he marveled.

Cascavel felt a slight twinge of conscience as he reflected on how this Max - Diego had given the *bandido* his name - had not demonstrated the least bit of malice toward him. He easily shook it off, however, when he remembered his new freedom. Now, in the space of one day, he had gone from street riffraff to special agent of the Cabritan government. He had even been given a uniform, and the promise that if he did well, there was promotion, power, and wealth in his future.

Cascavel was brought back to reality by the sight of a black Mercedes in the streets below navigating its way to the *Paladar Dourado.*

He put the walkie-talkie to his face. "The package has arrived."

"Very good," came the reply from Diego. "The operation is a go. Plant the bug."

So eager was Cascavel to begin his new mission that he failed to take note of the roof he was standing on. It was composed of ancient ceramic tiles, held together by force of habit, and when he applied pressure, they slipped out from under him, causing the surprised *bandido* to lose his balance. Crashing to the roof and sliding on his back, he grasped wildly for anything to stop his fall. His fingers closed around the walkie-talkie. With a yell - punctuated by the rows of tiles as he passed over them - Cascavel slid down the roof, over the gutter, and into a garbage can two stories below.

The *Paladar Dourado* occupied a building that had begun life as an armory, built by the Portuguese crown for the supply of the occupying troops. It was a solid, stone structure. Massive wooden beams, hand-hewn from jungle trees and pulled by slaves to the capital city, supported the edifice. After its military career had ended, the building had passed from one owner to another, until two brothers - immigrants from Italy - bought it and turned it into a restaurant. The first two floors were nice, but the *piece de resistance* was the terrace. There was no covering: customers dined under the stars. On rainy nights, dining was restricted to the first two floors.

The sky this night was crystal clear. Stars shone brilliantly, appearing to Max to be closer than usual. A quiet breeze blew, lightly fluttering the cloth napkins on the circular tables. In the corner a singer crooned Frank Sinatra classics, accompanied by a five-piece band.

Ilana indicated a table close to the edge of the terrace - one that would afford them both privacy and a stunning view of the city lights. They sat down. A waiter materialized, and they placed their orders. Then Ilana turned to Max.

"So, my mysterious friend, we've shopped together, eaten together, danced together, and thwarted a robbery together. And I don't know anything about you. I think at this point - especially after giving you a ride in my Mercedes - that I am entitled to a little information." Her tone was playful, but belied a real curiosity. Her eyes seemed larger as she leaned forward, elbows on the table, head in her hands, expectantly waiting.

Max sighed. Talking about himself was not his favorite pastime. But now he knew the moment of truth had arrived. Before sitting down, he had quickly scanned the surroundings to see if there were any other bugs in place. Being relatively assured of the privacy of their conversation, he had no excuse to delay further.

"My full name is Maxwell Sherman." He waited to see if that caused any reaction. It didn't. Max was relieved. "I grew up in and around New York City. My family is… fairly well-to-do. I guess I was pretty privileged. The downside of being the the only child of busy executives is that I did't get to play with many kids my age. The silver lining was that we had the United Nations living in our house, in the form of the servants.

"I don't follow."

Well, my Nanny was Venezuelan, the gardener was German, the butler was French, and the cook was Egyptian, so…"

"So you grew up speaking all those languages." Ilana filled in. Max nodded in the affirmative. "Was your chauffeur Portuguese?"

"No. Like I said, For that I took a crash course. But that's getting ahead of the story. The thing is, I pretty much took all that privilege for granted. If you knew me then, you would probably say that I was somewhat of a party animal."

"Really!" Ilana was incredulous. "You certainly don't seem like the 'millionaire playboy' type now. What happened?"

"Well, first off, when I was fifteen my Dad died in a car accident. We were close, despite his busy schedule. We would go on family vacations to our cabin near the Adirondacks, and Dad and I would have all kinds of adventures in the woods. When I was twelve I started getting interested in martial arts, and so he hired the best teachers and came to all of my competitions."

"That explains the scene with 'Snake.'"

Max smiled. "Partially. Anyway, when Dad died, I went off the deep end. I spun way out of control. I started hanging out with the bad crowd at school, and getting into fights just...just because I felt like fighting. Because of my training, some of those fights got pretty ugly, and the police got involved more than once. Mom was dealing with her grief my throwing herself into the family business, and she had no idea what to do with her berserk son. After high school she sent me to the best college their money could buy, thinking that it would shape me up. After about a year, though, it was pretty evident she was wasting her money."

Two blocks away, Cascavel swore and stood up in the trash can. He wiped the filth off his new uniform as best he could - which was not very well. Disgusted, he pocketed the walkie-talkie and jumped out of the can - right onto the tail of a passing cat. The angry feline let out a yowl and furiously scratched at Cascavel's leg, further jangling the *bandido's* already-frazzled nerves.

Taking a few deep breaths, he looked around him. He was in a back alley behind the house. The binoculars were, miraculously, still hanging around his neck.

His walkie-talkie crackled to life. "Everything okay there?"

Cascavel answered quickly. "Everything's fine. Just… ah… scouting out the right place to put the bug."

"Get to it! You don't have all night."

Swearing again as he clicked off the walkie-talkie, he stepped out into the street - just as a delivery truck passed by, soaking him from head to toe in water from a nearby puddle. Shaking with equal parts rage and cold, Cascavel stood there, looking very much like a drenched Chihuahua.

"So then what happened?" Ilana asked.

"As I was leaving the college dorm, I ran into an Army recruiter. He asked me what my goal in life was. I told him I was looking for some people to beat up. He smiled and invited me to his office. Within the week I was on my way to basic training. My mother went into a towering rage, but there was nothing she could do. My goal was to become a Green Beret, and three days after 9-11 happened that became a reality. I spent the next few years in Afghanistan, Iraq, and…other places."

"Ooh!" Ilana put down her fork and looked in wonder at her companion. "The man of mystery just got more mysterious." Max responded with a wry smile.

"Trust me, even if I could talk about them, I wouldn't. There are things that make me wake up at night in a cold sweat." He shook his head as if to rid it of unpleasant memories, then continued. "After the tour of duty in the middle east I was assigned to an anti-narcotics unit. In preparation for those assignments I was sent to a facility in the Amazon, run by the Brazilians, that specializes in training for jungle warfare."

"And that's where you got your 'crash course' in Portuguese."

"Exactly."

Ilana beheld the man across the table from her with admiration. She thought back to when she had first seen him in that marketplace. He seemed so different now - almost larger than life. Reflecting on their shared experiences over the last few days, she realized that when she was with him she felt a feeling of adventure, and yet of safety at the same time. How many other men had given her that feeling?

"None."

"None what?" asked Max.

"Er..." Flustered, Ilana realized she had answered her mental question out loud. "None... of this explains how you ended up here on Cabrito."

"Ah, well, Army life began to wear on me, and so I requested discharge. After I left, I had no direction and was pretty traumatized by some of the things I had seen. My mother was ecstatic when I came back and wanted me to jump right into an executive position at the company. The thought of sitting in an office in Manhattan all day made my stomach turn. Instead, I bummed around for a while, until I finally got a job at a construction company upstate, near Albany. The hard physical work helped to distract me from my memories. Once again my mother was... shall we say, peeved."

Despite his earlier mishap on the roof, Cascavel was really quite good at climbing things. Growing up on the streets of the *Paraíso* slums, he had survived primarily by shimmying up walls and running over rooftops to get away irate neighbors, rival gangs - whomever happened to be chasing him at the time. Thus, the restaurant wall before him posed no real challenge.

The ancient, vine-covered stone wall provided many hand- and toeholds. The wooden beams sticking out just below the terrace would provide the perfect platform for him to carry out his job. Without further delay, Cascavel began his ascent.

He chose the back wall of the building, where there were no windows. It would not do for anybody to see him. He began his gecko-like climb and was soon at the top. There he could hear the sounds of gentle music, light conversation, and the tinkling of ice in glasses.

Someday, I will be the one sitting at the table, listening to music, sipping wine in glasses that clink, he told himself. Then, he went back to work.

Supporting himself with one arm on one of the protruding wooden beams, he hoisted his wiry frame up so just the top part of his head appeared over the wall. To his delight he found he was almost completely hidden by decorative plants that surrounded the terrace. Peering through them, he also found that he had calculated with surprising precision - he was directly behind the table where the *americano* and the girl were sitting. Instinctively, he reached over to feel his arm... still sore from yesterday.

Ilana was about to sip her coffee when she stopped and sniffed the air. "Do you smell something funny?"

"The only thing I can smell is your perfume," replied Max, truthfully. It was intoxicating, making it hard for him to concentrate.

"No, seriously, I smell something... like... like garbage."

A gentle breeze blew through, and Max caught a whiff. "Oh my, now I smell it too. Wow, somebody needs to take out the trash."

Ilana shrugged. "Probably from the street below. Anyway, you were talking about what happened after you left the Army."

"Oh, right. Well, one Friday evening in February, about four years ago, I was walking from work to the little apartment I rented. I had been pretty much disowned by my family and really didn't care about anything or anybody. I was looking forward to a weekend of meaningless drinking - alone.

"No girlfriend?" Ilana asked slyly.

"Plenty of girls, none of them friends. Anyway, on the way to my apartment that night, I passed a little church I had passed many times before. It was getting dark, and I noticed that there was a light in the back of the building. Suddenly, my entire being longed for some sort of human contact. The warmth of the light beckoned to me. Before I knew what was happening, I was knocking on the door.

"A man answered and introduced himself as Pastor Dave. He invited me in, and we began to talk. It was casual at first, but he could tell all was not well with me. He began to gently probe, and suddenly I was pouring my entire, miserable life out to him."

Ilana was surprised to see Max's eyes become moist at the recollection.

"Then Pastor Dave began to talk to me about Jesus," Max continued. "I was pretty ignorant about Him... used His name a lot as a swear word. But Dave spoke about Him as if he and Jesus were intimate friends, in fact he even used the phrase 'best buds.' It was something completely new to me, but I was sure this guy had something going for him that I didn't.

"Before I left, he gave me a Bible and told me to read John and Romans. I went home, broke open a six-pack, and did just that. I never finished the six-pack, but by Saturday evening, I had finished John and Romans."

Ilana hoped the shock was not registering on her face as Max told his story. When Max had explained his church work she had assumed it was some sort of charitable, social thing. Never in her wildest dreams would she have taken Max for *religious*. He seemed too real, too at ease with himself. Apart from the Roman Catholicism of the island, her contact with Christians had been the intellectual, academic Christianity of the American university campus, and the reason for its existence seemed to be connected to one political cause or another.

The man in front of her was expressing something far different.

Cascavel had a plan. He would carefully reach over and place the microphone in the plants next to him. From there, it would capture the conversation just fine. Still supporting himself by his arm on the wooden beam, he reached with his other hand and found the small mic. Hoisting himself up, he knelt on the beam and turned the appliance on. A red light blinked encouragingly. *Now to place it in the shrubbery...*

Suddenly, the *bandido* felt that something was very wrong. Unbeknownst to him, the nylon cord from which the binoculars hung had looped around the wooden beam while he was watching the couple through the shrubbery. Now, as he went to stand up, the cord pulled taut, and Cascavel lost his balance. With a yelp, he toppled over. Clawing at his neck, he grabbed the cord with one hand and found himself dangling by it, two stories above the street.

Ilana was lifting a fork full of delicious stroganoff to her tantalizing - as Max would have described them - lips when she paused.

"Did you hear something?"

"No, did you?"

"I think so... it sounded like a yell."

"Probably from the kitchen. Maybe somebody got burned."

"Could be," replied Ilana. "So, Pastor Dave told you to read John and Romans. What about them made such an impression on you?" She was genuinely interested.

Max chuckled. "Pastor Dave knew what he was doing. When I read John, I met Jesus. I saw his humanity, his deity, his love, his goodness... John has it all. Then in Romans, I learned of my condition before God. I saw clearly that I stood guilty before a righteous God, a God who could not let my evil deeds go unpunished."

"That's a scary idea of God. Isn't that somewhat outdated?"

"I always thought so," Max admitted. "But I came to see that what was important was whether or not it was true, not whether or not it was fashionable."

Ilana did not reply, so Max pressed on.

"Anyway, on Sunday morning I went to church. One verse that I had read was burning in my head. 'If you confess with your mouth the Lord Jesus, and believe in your heart that God has raised him from the dead, you will be saved.' And at that point, it all came together. I realized that there was absolutely nothing I could do to please God - that Jesus had already accomplished that for me two thousand years ago on the cross. I just needed to embrace that in faith and allow it to have its effect on my life."

Ilana sighed. "What you have sounds really beautiful. But I'm too used to solving problems with my mind. Your belief is obviously helping you, but it won't work for me."

"So what you are saying is that religion may be good for us common folk, but for educated people like yourself it is not necessary." Max gave her a sly wink.

"No, silly, that is not what I am saying... not really!" She made a playful swipe at him.

"I'm just teasing," he replied. "Hey, the food was delicious, but it's getting late. How about I let you take me home?"

"Okay. But thanks for telling me your story. It is really... beautiful."

Max smiled. The old Max would have said, "Not as beautiful as you," or some other cheap pick-up line. The new Max, however, was more interested in Ilana meeting Jesus. There was much more Max wanted to say to her, but it went unsaid as they made their way to the stairway.

Once again, Cascavel pulled himself to the top of the terrace. Slowly he reached for the tiny microphone and stood up gingerly on the wooden beam, this time making sure there was nothing around his neck. Then he carefully placed the microphone in the shrubbery, peered through the leaves… and softly swore. The girl and the *gringo* were gone!

Nearby, two waiters, one tall and lanky and the other short and portly, cleaned off a table where several businessmen had been dining.

"José, watch your language, man!" said the tall waiter to his co-worker.

"You watch *your* language, man! I didn't say anything."

"Forget it. What should I do with the beer they left in this mug?"

"Just throw it in the shrubbery."

Before Cascavel knew what was happening, he found himself drenched by a liter of vintage *cabritana* brew. As the potent liquid ran down his face and neck, it came into contact with the cuts and bruises he had sustained from his earlier mishaps. Forgetting himself, he put his hands over the sore spots… and in doing so, once again lost his balance. Arms flailing, he fell from the beam. Fortunately, the binoculars were still hanging from the beam by their nylon cord, and for the second time that night Cascavel found himself swinging helplessly in the night air.

"Hello, Cascavel, are you there?" The voice was coming from the walkie-talkie in his pocket. In frustration, Cascavel grabbed it with his free hand and hurled it to the pavement far below, where it broke into a hundred tiny pieces.

A VOICE IN THE DARKNESS

Max and Ilana stood in front of the Blakes' house. She looked up at him, her eyes aglow.

"I had a wonderful time."

"So did I," Max replied. There was a moment of silence, pregnant with anticipation. Max took Ilana's hand in his, and gently placed a small Bible in her palm.

"Read..."

"I know, I know. John and Romans." She completed his phrase with a wink. "You know, when I went on dates in the US, the guys usually tried to give me something else at the door. This is the first time I have gotten a Bible." She paused. "A little unorthodox, but sweet, nonetheless." With that she turned, got in her car, and sped off.

As the tail lights of the Mercedes disappeared into the night, Max reflected on their evening. He remembered that as he had told her his story, Ilana had hung on his every word. Involuntarily, he contrasted this with the time he'd spent with Mary Sue, where she did most of the talking.

Stop making those comparisons! he reprimanded himself. They are only going to get you in trouble.

Max closed the gate behind him and made his way across the lawn to the darkened house. It had been an eventful day, and tomorrow was going to be even more so.

Truly exhausted, he placed his key into the front door... and froze. Something was amiss. Max knew he had locked the door before he left - and now it was unlocked.

His senses once again on full alert, he slowly entered the room.

"Good evening, Max." The voice came from the darkness. "I hope you don't mind that I let myself in."

Back at the warehouse down by the docks, it took all the self-control Diego had to suppress the rage welling up within him as he listened to Cascavel's report. *Stupid! Incompetent! And...*

"You stink."

"I am sorry, *senhor* Diego. If you will give me another chance..."

"No, I mean you really stink. You smell of garbage and beer and..." Diego sniffed, "...cat?" With superhuman effort, Diego calmed himself. He motioned to a bathroom at the other end of the warehouse. "Go shower in there. I need to figure out what our next step will be."

Max relaxed and closed the door behind him. "Mr. Rockwell. It's been a long time."

"That it has," replied the voice in the darkness. "And please, call me Jim." A soft *click*, and a flame appeared. Max could barely make out Mr. Rockwell's - Jim's - face in the flicker from the cigarette lighter.

"Those things will kill you, you know." Max reached over and turned on the light. James Rockwell was sitting comfortably in an easy-chair. He smiled warmly.

"I rather think the stress of the job is going to get me first. A stress, I might add, that your presence here has increased exponentially."

"It's nice to see you, too," said Max, flopping down on the nearby sofa.

The older man chuckled. "Imagine my surprise when I watched you walk into that ballroom," he said. "You were absolutely the last person I was expecting to see here."

"Well, if it is any comfort, you caused me a bit of a shock as well. Seriously, I had no idea."

"I kind of figured that," said James. "I was very curious as to what strange winds had brought you here, until I saw your companion. I must say, your taste in women has improved. So, did you meet her in the US? In the Army? On the Internet?"

"None of the above. I actually met her after I arrived. And, for your information, we are not an item."

"Perhaps not in your mind, but I saw the way she looked at you as you swept her around the dance floor. She's quite smitten."

James' observation made Max uneasy. His thoughts turned from Ilana to Mary Sue, and back to Ilana again. In fact, it was becoming harder and harder to think of Mary Sue without thinking of Ilana, as his dream the previous night had made painfully clear. He would have to work that through later; James was talking again.

"So what brings you to Cabrito anyway?"

Max regarded the man in front of him. There was a long history between them, but nothing that should make Max wary of him. Yet he remembered that at the ball James had been seated next to Dr. Santana - and he was becoming more and more convinced that Santana was somehow behind the arson of the church building, not to mention the sudden departure of the Blakes. He decided to limit the information he gave to Mr. Rockwell.

"Suffice it to say, it has nothing to do with why you are here. Up until yesterday, I had no idea that SPGI was opening a division here."

"Well, that certainly puts me more at ease," replied James. "Although, you must understand that my... ah... superiors will be very interested in your presence here."

"I bet she will," responded Max. "I assume she already knows."

"Oh, of course. Don't be surprised if you get a visit."

"Why would I get a visit now when a week ago I was living within driving distance?"

"I think you may underestimate her desire for your wellbeing."

"Given our history, can you see why I might be a little skeptical?"

Rockwell chuckled. "All of this is really none of my business. The only purpose for my visit is to make sure that nothing will impede me from the fulfillment of the duties for which I am paid."

"You could have called."

"You're right, but this way the effect was much more dramatic, no?"

"So, would you like something to drink before you go?"

"No, thank you. I'll show myself to the door."

And with that, James Rockwell was gone.

Raymond Sand lived in a house that had once been the mansion of the Alvares family, one of the original big landowners of Cabrito. The family - and the house - had fallen on hard times, and by the time Ray was looking to settle down on the island, the once-proud mansion was in shambles and available for a pittance. Now that the American expat had lived there for over twenty years, the condition of the house was not remarkably better. The lawn was unkempt, the veranda was cluttered with junk, and the upstairs windows gave the impression of disuse.

It was late at night when Ray followed the well-worn tracks to the back of the house, where stood what had once been a stable. He got out of the yellow taxi, opened the double wooden doors, and drove inside. Cars of various makes and models, in varying states of disrepair, lined both sides of the long building. Ray parked the VW in the only empty slot, got out, and gazed with satisfaction at his collection. A '57 Chevy, a '72 Mustang, an ancient Model T, a '39 Mercedes with "suicide" doors. And in the back, covered by an olive-green tarp, his *magnum opus*.

Over the years, he had bought junked vehicles on the cheap and spent his spare hours tinkering with them. There was something about the whole process - puttering with the tools, fitting the right piece into the right slot, feeling the grease underneath his fingernails - that was relaxing and made him temporarily forget the sadness that usually overwhelmed him.

And when mechanics didn't work, the bourbon did.

Turning off the light and reluctantly shutting the door on his trophy case, Ray trudged to the back door of his house. He went to the kitchen and poured himself a glass of water. He was tired from his stakeout, confused by what he had just seen, and wanted to do nothing more than sleep. But questions kept crowding into his head.

Why had Max decided to stay? Why was the government so interested in getting rid of him? Why was Ilana involved in this? And, most recently, why had the American from SPGI paid Max a visit this evening?

The old man shook his head as if to expel the unwanted thoughts, then reached into his cupboard for some sleeping pills. As he ingested three of them at once, his eye caught the label on the bottle, and he stopped, mid-swallow.

Sherman Pharmaceutical Group, International

Sherman. Maxwell *Sherman*. Ray shook his head.

Probably just a coincidence, he thought. But the more he reflected, the more he realized the odds were against coincidence.

Thoughtfully, he shuffled into his bedroom. While this flash of insight did not reveal the whole picture, it was definitely a big piece to the puzzle.

Not that it really mattered much. Dr. Santana and company probably had that connection all figured out already. Right now, there was work to do. He walked over to a corner and picked up a pile of old magazines. Setting them on the table, he found a pair of scissors and carefully began cutting out letters.

CHAPTER 15

DIFFERENCES OF OPINION

By the time the next day rolled around, Max had come to the conclusion that, if he planned on being of any use to the people of the little congregation, he needed to study two things: the language and the Bible.

Of the two, perfecting his Portuguese and learning Kryollo would be the easier. As he had explained to Ilana, languages came easy for him, and this natural ability had been honed during his time as a Green Beret. It would simply be a matter of brushing up on his Portuguese adding the native Kryollo of the Cabritans to his current repertoire of Spanish, French, German, Farsi, Hebrew, and, of course, English.

Learning enough about the Bible to be any kind of spiritual leader to the fledgling congregation - now that would be the real challenge. Since his conversion four years prior, Max had attended weekly one-on-one Bible studies with Pastor Dave. The young minister had a way of making the Bible come alive, and Max always came away from those sessions with the unique sensation of being both satisfied and desperately hungry for more. Always a voracious reader, Max had pored over the sacred text daily since his conversion. His fellow construction workers had snickered as he read his Bible during lunch breaks - although always at a safe distance and downwind. Yet the more he read, the more he realized he was just scratching the surface.

How am I ever going to be any kind of help to these people if I am such an amateur myself?

Fortunately, the left-behind library of Mr. Blake provided some help. It contained works on systematic theology, a couple commentaries on the entire Bible, and many other books of interest - including a basic introduction to New Testament Greek.

Over the next few days, Max settled into somewhat of a routine. Upon awaking, he would spend the first hours of the day - until lunch - in study. Oriented by his recently-acquired library, he devoured the Bible with renewed intensity. He also did daily exercises from a small Cabritan Kryollo textbook.

After lunch he would embark on "fact-finding missions" into the city. On his first forays out he was usually accompanied by either Bernardinho or his daughter, Isabela. He soon had the confidence to strike out on his own, however, and did so with relish.

As the days wore on, he realized that he was growing to love Santo Expedito. The narrow, winding streets of the *Cidade Antiga* - the old colonial section - contrasted with the wide avenues and block-like structures of the more modern downtown area, the sidewalk cafés where old men sat around and swapped stories, the fish markets by the sea - life here moved at its own slow, lackadaisical pace.

Max was always discovering nooks and crannies that were cultural treasure troves. On his third trip into the old section of town, he was delighted to find a large, if musty, used book store. There, he encountered numerous titles - in English and Portuguese - on the history and culture of his new home. There was even a volume on the Yamani tribe, apparently written by an eighteenth-century British missionary. The man gave a detailed - if less than complementary description of the customs of Ilana's people. He described their tribal divisions, rituals, and customs, some of which gruesome to read. Max smiled, trying to imagine the beautiful, educated woman he knew, growing up in that milieu.

The British missionary also theorized as to the origin of the Yamani language, observing certain similarities between it and the Ute-Aztec language group. This made Max wonder how they had arrived on this island, how long ago they had made the overseas trip, and what had motivated their move. He made a mental note to ask Ilana about it later.

And as he thought about Ilana, his mind wandered to a conversation they had had on the previous Sunday. It after the evening service at the Igreja da Paz. As he greeted people after the message, Max was pleased to note that Ray had attended every week since that first Sunday. He sat in the back and didn't interact at all with the others, and then he left as soon as possible when it was over. But the young American was hopeful that the message might be having its effect on the older man. And on that Sunday Ilana had appeared. There had been only sporadic contact between them since their dinner on the terrace. Max had been busy with his self-education and the details of leading the small congregation, and Ilana with preparations for the upcoming indigenous festival.

Now she was sitting with the rest of the congregation, and it took every ounce of self-control for Max to concentrate on his message. He had to force himself to remember that there were other people in the audience besides the beautiful creature sitting three rows back, two seats from the aisle.

When the service was over, she was the first one to greet him.

"Will you have time to talk later?"

"I'll make time."

Ilana flashed him her infectious smile. Out of the corner of his eye, Max saw Ray regarding them with a strange expression on his face. He excused himself and tried to make his way over to where the older man was standing. But by the time he got there, Ray had ducked out the door, and all Max heard was the sound of the retreating VW Beetle.

Later, when most of the crowd had dissipated, Max and Ilana sat facing each other on a couple of the folding chairs that served as pews for the congregation.

"So, Missionary Max," she began, referring to the title everybody at the congregation used for him. Max winced and she laughed. "I have been reading the Bible you gave me."

"And?"

"And there is a lot I don't understand. But a couple things are really bothering me."

"Such as?"

"Well, for starters, the part where Jesus says he is *the* way, *the* truth, *the* life. I have no problem thinking of him as *a* way to life… but the kind of exclusivity he is claiming is offensive to me."

"And why is it offensive?"

"Well, if you really believe that, then you think that my people of the Yamani tribe are condemned to an eternity in Hell. Is that true?" Her voice held an accusatory tone.

"Not just them, but everybody who is without Christ." Max could tell that this was not the answer she had been hoping for.

"Listen here, you… you American, Christian… *paternalist!*" Her black eyes flashed in challenge.

She's even beautiful when she's ticked off, Max reflected.

"The Yamani are a noble race, not primitive savages. They are made up of three tribes that have a complex system of government and a vibrant society - much like the six Iroquois nations from your home state."

"The Iroquois might not be the best example to use," Max observed. "Sure they had an impressive civil government, but they also brutally killed men, women, and children and ate the flesh and drank the blood of their enemies."

"But… but these things are culturally determined. Those practices were part of their culture and should be respected."

Max's eyebrows went up. "All the same, I think I prefer not to be on the menu." Then, remembering the reading he had done recently about the Yamani tribes, "I trust your people have abandoned their own cannibalistic tendencies."

Ilana flushed a deep red. "That is pretty smug coming from an American. From what I hear, abortion is still legal in the US."

"Unfortunately. And if I were trying to defend American culture, then you might have a point. But I'm not. You read where

Jesus said that He is the way, the truth, and the life. The farther any people strays from Him, the more barbaric become their practices - whether it be cannibalism or the wholesale slaughter of innocents."

Ilana was silent for some time. Max was afraid he had not helped the situation at all. Finally she spoke. "The other problem I have is with Christ's death. Why was that necessary? Couldn't God have done the whole redemption process without that? I mean, he's God, right? He makes the rules. Surely he could have come up with a less horrific method of atonement."

"That's actually a question I had for a long time," Max replied. "I finally came to see that for God to demonstrate His love for us, it was necessary to satisfy His justice. The only one who could possibly do this was God, in the person of Jesus Christ. That is why what happened at the cross is so important. It was there that God's justice and His love are reconciled, once and for all."

Once again, Ilana fell silent. Then she said, "I have a lot to think about. But," and here her face brightened considerably, "I insist that you come to our tribal celebration. Perhaps then you will be convinced that my people are not evil savages." Then she looked at him slyly. "And don't worry, you will not be on the menu. Those traditions died out with the arrival of the white man. Although, if you don't behave, I can have a little talk with the tribal cooks..."

Max chuckled, relieved that they were still friends. "I think they would find me a little lean."

Ilana giggled and then stood up to leave. "The festival starts on Wednesday. Be at the airport at 7 a.m. The FUNAPI helicopter will be there to take you to the celebration grounds."

Now it was Tuesday evening. Max had spent a little longer on his explorations than normal, and the shadows were growing long as he made his way on foot toward his home. On several occasions during these explorations, he had sensed that he was being followed. He was under no illusions that whoever it was that wanted him off the island had given up. Yet for the last four weeks they had done nothing overt, and for that he was grateful.

Grateful, and perhaps a little careless. As he walked along a deserted street, he was suddenly grabbed from behind by someone with an iron grip. Instinct kicked in, and he was about to execute a Judo throw when he felt the unmistakable jab of a firearm in his back.

"*Calma aí, mano.*" The low voice spoke Portuguese… but not with the Cabritan accent. The slang and the soft flowing tone were familiar to him from his time spent in jungle warfare training in the Amazon.

Whoever it was was pushed him into a dimly-lit alley, and there Max came face-to-face with a very large man holding a very large machine gun - pointed straight at him.

"Be calm, and nothing will happen to you. We don't want to hurt you." The accent was the same. *Definitely Brazilian*, thought Max. "Right, no hurting," the man behind him echoed.

Without taking his eyes - or his gun - off Max, the man in front of him brought his free hand up and spoke into a tiny walkie-talkie, which was made even tinier by the hugeness of the man's hand.

"We've got him," he said.

"Right. We've got him." Again the echo from the man behind him.

"Good," came curt reply. Max was sure the voice on the walkie-talkie was female. A black sedan pulled up in front of the ally. The door opened, and a tall, severely beautiful woman stepped out. Her blond hair fell in perfectly formed waves around her shoulders, and when she walked toward them, it was as if she were on a catwalk at a fashion show. Her high heels clicked firmly on the cobblestones, and she approached with the self-assured poise of someone completely in control of the situation.

She stepped up to Max and looked him in the eye. Max was trying to remember where he had seen this woman before. Paris? Milan? A movie?

"Why are you in Cabrito?" The question was posed in English, but with an accent that made the words drip off her tongue in a most exotic way.

"Um… it's a long story, and better told without a gun in my back."

A slight movement of her head, and the man behind Max released his grip. He moved around to the front, and Max saw him for the first time. He was almost a carbon copy of his companion - wearing an identical overcoat and carrying an identical weapon.

"Now, tell me why you are here." There was no hint of suggestion in the woman's voice. Noting that the two guns were still leveled at him, Max took a deep breath and told her, as quickly as possible, the reason for his presence on the island. When he was finished, there was a pause while the woman considered what he had said.

"You are aware, are you not, that my husband wants you off of this island." There was an unhidden contempt in the way she pronounced *husband*, and suddenly Max remembered where he had seen her. The woman before him was none other than Francesca, the Brazilian supermodel wife of Emídio Santana. He had seen her at the gala and had noticed the same cold contempt for her husband then.

"That's the impression I've been getting," Max replied. "Any idea why?"

Francesca rolled her eyes. "He is like a god on this island. I know very little of his business, but I do know that for some reason he is very interested in the Yamani Indians. It cannot be out of any real love for them, for he loves only himself. It is more likely that he and his father have some enterprise that somehow depends on nobody interfering with them. You need to be very careful. I know that the other missionaries tried to work with the Yamanis, and suddenly they received threats on their lives and the lives of their children. I know my husband was involved somehow."

The two machine guns trained on him notwithstanding, Max began to get the impression that he was dealing with a friend.

"Why are you telling me all of this?" he asked.

"For two reasons. Number one, I hate my husband." The words were spoken matter-of-factly, without emotion.

"Second, because you are a missionary. When I was a little girl in the interior Minas Gerais - it's a state in Brazil - an American missionary came to our little town and started a Baptist church. My family went, and those were the happiest years of my life. Then I decided to seek fame and fortune, and it got me... this." She motioned to her surroundings. "Don't get me wrong. I love Cabrito - it is life with Emídio that I hate. But I would hate it more if he succeeded in frightening away another missionary."

Max started to reply, but she held a finger to his mouth. "Don't speak, just listen. They are plotting ways to get you out of here. They will stop at nothing. They will not hesitate to cause you physical harm, or to kill you. I heard what you did to the *bandido* on the street..."

How did she hear about that? Max wondered.

"...and so it is obvious that you know how to take care of yourself. But they are many, and you cannot defeat them all, all of the time. I have instructed my trusted bodyguards, Itamar and Inácio, to keep an eye on you." She indicated the two men standing nearby.

"Hello," said Itamar.

"Right, hello," echoed Inácio.

"Hi." Max waved, tentatively. His mysterious benefactor continued. "They have been with me since I was a model in Brazil. They are very loyal, and very... effective. But be careful - even they cannot be everywhere at once."

"We can't," agreed Itamar.

"Right, we can't," echoed Inácio.

She paused a moment, then continued.

"Emídio is also quite enamored with your little Indian girlfriend."

This woman knows everything, Max thought, and then, *She's not my girlfriend!* He decided this was not the time to protest the point.

"Know this," Francesca continued. "He uses women and then throws them away. It will be no different with her. If you care at all for her, you will do everything you can to keep him away from her."

With that, Francesca turned and walked away, her heels clicking sharply on the sidewalk. Itamar and Inácio, who had lowered their weapons, each gave Max a friendly pat on the shoulder as they followed her to the car.

"Be careful."

"Right. Very careful."

Once they were all inside, the car sped off into the night, leaving a slightly bewildered Max with a lot to think about.

CHAPTER 16

GOING NATIVE

Dr. Emídio Santana sat, cross-legged, on the ground. Despite the lack of chairs, his position was one of honor, as it was at the chiefs' table of the Yamani celebration. Before him was spread all manner of jungle delicacies - fruits, vegetables, jungle wildlife of different varieties - and this was only breakfast. Having attended such festivals before, Santana knew that the food would be continually replenished throughout the day.

To Santana's right sat the *presidente*, and to his left, Mr. Rockwell. Behind him, ever watchful, stood Diego. The three tribes who, combined, formed the Yamani Confederation had already begun their celebration. The tree-dwellers were doing the traditional welcome dance, while the land-dwellers and rock-dwellers waited their turn.

But Emídio Santana was hardly paying attention to the festivities. He had eyes only for Ilana. She was dressed in the traditional garb of her tribe, and Santana was transfixed. His eyes devoured her every movement. Here she was, in the jungle, and there was nothing standing in his way. No social concerns, no Francesca, and no stupid American.

The thought of the American drew him up short. He leaned over to President Ferraz.

"I trust the American missionary situation is being dealt with."

"Oh, indeed. All the legal aspects have been covered and…"

"You know I could care less about the legal aspects! I just want him off the island. My own attempts, thus far, have been… unsuccessful." He cast a quick glance at Diego, who shifted uncomfortably.

"Trust me, Dr. Santana," said Ferraz. "You will never see the face of this American again. He will be… "

He was interrupted by the sound of an approaching helicopter. The dancers on the field stopped mid-step to look at the flying machine as it slowly descended into the jungle clearing. The symbol of FUNAPI was clearly visible on the side.

Then the eyes of the guests of honor widened as the door opened and out jumped Maxwell Sherman.

Dr. Santana looked at the president, who in turn was staring, mouth agape, at the American. "You were saying?"

"Um… well… I…" There were really no words that could express the mortification Osvaldo Ferraz felt at that moment. It had all been planned so well. The military police were to arrive at his house that morning with official deportation papers, effective immediately. Ray the taxi driver would be there to take him, if he went willingly. If not, there was a police van. He had even planned for it to occur while there would be no way of contacting them. If anybody complained later - say, the members of the church or the American government - he could claim that he knew nothing of it as, unfortunately, he was away on official business at the time.

So what was Max doing *here*? In his mind, President Ferraz could see the police arriving to an empty house. Finally, he managed to blurt, to nobody in particular, "I want to know who invited him!"

His question was answered immediately as Ilana ran up to him, gave him a hug, and planted a kiss on his cheek.

Max, ignorant of the drama that his appearance provoked among the elites, was a little perplexed at the sight of Ilana. Used to seeing her in a "civilized" context, he was unprepared for how she looked in the garb of her people. She was dressed in a simple, one-piece dress made of what appeared to be the skin of a leopard. Her ankles and wrists were adorned with bands made of the same material. On her head was an extravagant feather headdress. Every inch of exposed skin - arms, legs, face, neck - was painted with intricate geometric designs. A necklace made of bones, teeth, and other trinkets completed the ensemble.

Suddenly Max realized that he had been staring. Ilana stood before him, that same sly smile on her face. "What do you think?" she asked.

"I think perhaps I came underdressed," Max said. "At the very least I need a paint job."

She laughed and grabbed his hand. "Come on! The dance of the land-dwellers - that's my tribe - is about to start. I saved you a spot next to the *presidente.*"

She led him over to where the others were sitting. "Mr. President, Dr. Santana, I want you to meet my friend Max."

"Olá!" Max said cheerily, noticing the profound discomfort his presence was causing them.

The two men responded with unenthusiastic, monosyllabic greetings. The look on Santana's face was positively poisonous.

"And this is Mr. Rockwell, who is here with SPGI."

"Nice to meet you, Mr. Rockwell," he said, affecting ignorance.

Rockwell gave him a meaningful glance. "The pleasure is all mine."

If Ilana noticed anything odd about the exchange, she paid no mind. "You sit here and enjoy the show. I'll be back after my people have finished their presentation." With that, Ilana skipped back to where her tribespeople were gathered.

An icy silence reigned at the table. The president and Santana glared at Max. Mr. Rockwell shifted uncomfortably.

This is going to be delightful, thought Max. He turned his attention to the proceedings in front of him.

One thing was for sure: the Yamani tribes had gone all-out for this festival. Each group presented an intricate routine involving men, women, and children. Feet drummed, feathers swished, and voices raised in chant. After each tribe was finished, all of them joined together for a grand finale. The men of each group approached the center, spears leveled, fierce expressions on their face. Around them the women and children formed a circle, beating on drums and uttering harrowing screams which Max felt certain were war cries.

The posturing and screaming was quickly reaching a crescendo. Suddenly Ilana ran into the middle of the three groups of men. Silence fell. Softly, she began to sing a slow, haunting melody. A solitary drum began to beat, and she swayed gently with the rhythm as she sang. Max could not understand the words, but the melody was sad, melancholic. As she sang, the rhythm picked up, and her gyrations became more and more pronounced.

It was then that Max noticed three warriors, one from each group, approaching her on soft feet. As she sang, they crept closer and closer. Then, her song reached its high point, and suddenly she stopped. The warrior from the tree-dwellers drew back his spear. Max caught his breath. The warrior lunged straight at Ilana, and at the same time there was a sharp beat on the drum.

Ilana deftly moved to one side, and the spear narrowly missed her. The warrior remained in position, his spear outstretched.

Another drum beat, and the rock-dweller warrior lunged. Again, Ilana stepped deftly aside, and the spear passed her harmlessly - although much too closely for Max's comfort. That warrior too remained in position, his spear crossing with the spear of the first warrior.

Finally, after what seemed like an eternity, the drum beat again and the land-dweller warrior lunged, barely missing Ilana, who was now in the center of a triangle of spears. The drum began to beat again, slowly, and Ilana turned and twisted within the triangle. As she turned, she slowly sank to her knees, then fell to the ground, arm outstretched.

There was a pause, and then a shout went up from the crowd. The three warriors stuck their spears into the ground around the fallen maiden. The drums began a joyful, rhythmic beat and the warriors began to leap and jump around her, as if in great celebration. All the warriors then broke ranks and mixed with each other, finally forming a large circle around the three dancing warriors and the fallen girl. Then the women and children formed another, larger circle around them. The shouts were now of celebration.

To Max the story could not have been clearer. Three warring tribes were brought together by the selfless sacrifice of a jungle princess. It was beautiful and tragic at the same time. Though he knew it was all playacting, he had to admit that he felt a sense of relief when he saw Ilana get up and rejoin the dancing.

When Ilana joined the guests, she sat down next to Max and explained to him the details about the performance he had just witnessed.

"She was a land-people princess named Ilanamihi. That is actually my name too. Ilana is just easier to say."

"What does it mean?"

Ilana blushed. "Beautiful princess."

"It fits." This made her blush even more.

"Anyway, she grew tired of the warring between the peoples. One day, in the middle of a battle where all three tribes were fighting against each other, she ran out into the middle of the battlefield. She was immediately struck down by three spears, one from each tribe. The battle stopped as the soldiers looked on in horror at what they had done. Then they laid down their weapons and vowed never to go to war with each other again. This spot became the hallowed meeting place of all the tribes.

"You mean the battle took place right here?"

"This very clearing. And the place where I did the dance of Ilanamihi, that is, according to tradition, the very spot the original Ilanamihi was killed."

"This is fascinating!" Max exclaimed.

"The dance?"

"Well, that too. But I find it more interesting that someone who has a story like this in their cultural background would have such a hard time understanding the purpose of the death of Christ." Max could tell he had made an impression. He continued. "The princiess Ilanaweehee…"

"Ilanamihi."

"Right. Her. She died as a substitute for all the people who would have died in future wars. Christ died as a substitute for us, so we would not have to face the wrath of God. And, like Ilana… Ilanamal…"

"Ilanamihi."

"Exactly. Just like she reconciled her people to each other, Christ, by his death, reconciled us to God."

Ilana furrowed her brow. "But… there are a lot of differences in the two situations."

"Oh, absolutely!" said Max. "Unfortunately, the poor princess did not rise again. And her death only reconciled warring tribes. Christ, by his death, made peace between a rebellious creation and their righteous Creator."

Ilana shook her head. "You seem so convinced - but there's a lot I don't understand. After the reading I did, I still have a lot of questions."

"If it makes you feel any better, I still have some too. Right now I want to know exactly what it is I am eating!"

"Okay, let me see. Whatever you do, don't eat the red stuff."

"Why not?" Max asked.

"Just… take my word for it."

CHAPTER 17

RUMBLE IN THE JUNGLE

Despite the obvious ill will displayed toward him by his table companions, Max was having the time of his life. The morning dances were followed by a sumptuous lunch, and then the tribes divided up for spirited competition. Men and boys tested their athletic prowess by lifting logs, chasing wild pigs, and shooting targets with their bows and blowguns.

Then came the wrestling match. Two by two the tribesmen paired off and tried to pin each other down, accompanied by the hoots and hollers of their friends. The winner would strut around the circle for a few minutes then challenge another man. If the challenged demonstrated any hesitation, he was showered with derision until he was forced to accept.

One man - Ilana told Max his name was Kwah Len - won four fights in a row. Full of confidence and eating up the cheers of his friends, he strutted like a rooster around the circle. Then, to Max's great consternation, Kwah Len turned and pointed directly at him. The crowd grew quiet.

Ilana confirmed Max's fears: "He wants to wrestle you!"

"Is there any way I can get out of it?"

"I don't think so."

Reluctantly Max stood up. He took off his shirt and kicked off his tennis shoes. Not wanting to get holes in his socks, he pulled those off too.

"Just go a couple rounds with him and fall down," Ilana advised. "He won't rough you up too bad."

"Thanks a lot," replied Max as he walked to the middle of the ring. Kwah Len awaited him there, clearly anxious to add the white man to his growing list of vanquished foes. There were hoots and catcalls as the two men approached each other. Clearly this was going to be a major event for the tribe. Out of the corner of his eye, Max noticed that even the women - who for the most part had been ignoring the macho display - were inching toward the circle to get a better look.

Go a couple rounds and fall down, Max thought to himself as he watched his challenger circle him, milking the attention for all it was worth.

Suddenly Kwah Len lunged, and Max's training took over. Without thinking, his hand snaked out with lightning speed and grabbed the arm of his assailant. A quick twist, a scoop with his foot, a lift, a release - and a very surprised Yamani man went flying through the air. He landed with a *thud* on his back, and lay there, winded, for a few seconds. A momentary silence fell over the crowd, then they broke out in a cacophony of cheers, jeers, and raucous laughter. Obviously, they had been immensely entertained. Max looked over at Ilana and shrugged. She smiled her encouragement to him. Briefly, he caught a glimpse of Santana: he sat stony-faced, his eyes cold and calculating.

Meanwhile, Kwah Len got unsteadily to his feet. Shaking his head to clear it, he moved again toward his opponent - this time with a newfound respect. Slowly he circled his prey, looking for an opening. Then, without warning, he lunged for Max's middle. Taken off-guard by the move, Max felt himself falling backwards. Once again he went into autopilot, lifting his feet to his opponent's middle even as he fell, then, using his body as the fulcrum, pushing off as he hit the ground. Once again the hapless Kwah Len found himself hurtling through the air.

When Kwah Len hit the ground, Max was already up. Kwah Len scrambled to his feet and charged his foe. *Better put an end to this here,* Max decided as the wiry native approached him at full tilt. When Kwah Len was almost upon him - past the point where he could stop or change direction - Max set his feet and sprang. He caught Kwah Len around the middle, spun him around, then flipped him up over his shoulders. Both of them landed on the ground. In a flash, Max was on top of a prone Kwah Len, holding his arm behind his back.

Once again the crowd erupted. Max got up and helped Kwah Len to his feet. Other than a dusty stomach and damaged pride, he was fine. Max offered his hand, and the Yamani man took it. Then Max embraced him in the manner he had observed at the end of other fights. More cheers filled the air.

Then, as Kwah Len made his way back to the outer rim of the circle to face the jabs and teasing of his comrades, another chant began to rise. Max looked over and, to his shock, saw Emídio Santana standing there, shirtless and shoeless, a deadly look in his eyes.

The natives were shouting three syllables over and over again: *ka pho TWAN! ka pho TWAN!*

"It means," said Santana as he strode confidently towards Max, "let the white men fight."

Back in Santo Expedito, Ray leaned against his taxi, surrounded by military police. They had waited an hour in front of the American's house, and still there was no sign of Max. The sun was hot, and it was obvious that the officers with him would rather be somewhere else. They had arrived with a warrant for Max's arrest and immediate deportation. Ray was there to convince Max to go quietly.

The grounds, Ray had discovered in the course of their wait, were that Max had allegedly assaulted a citizen of Cabrito - a citizen who went by the name of Cascavel. Of course Ray knew that was hogwash, but as he had as much interest in Max leaving as anybody did, he made no protest.

But now Ray found himself relieved that Max wasn't home and hoping the police would decide to leave soon. He was way overdue for some R-and-R at the *Macaco Verde*.

Just as the cops were deciding to leave, they noticed a man walking toward them. Ray recognized him as Bernardinho.

"Is there some problem?" he asked, looking around at the police. Ray jumped in quickly, before any of the officers could respond.

"You don't happen to know where he is, do you?"

"He told me yesterday he was going to the jungle to watch a Yamani festival. Is there some problem?"

"Maybe. There is word on the street of a threat on Missionary Max's life," he lied. "I came with the police so they could ask him some questions."

Bernardinho sighed. "I was afraid of something like this." He fished inside his shirt for a moment, and then withdrew a folded envelope. Handing it to Ray, he said, "I received this a few days ago."

Ray took the envelope and opened it, although there was really no need. He already knew what was inside. The police officers crowded around him, and one of them read the words, words made of letters cut haphazardly from magazines and newspapers:

"Your family is in danger every day Missionary Max stays on Cabrito."

"I never told Missionary Max about this," Bernardinho continued softly. "We talked about it and decided that having him here with us was worth the risk."

"Interesting." The comment came from one of the officers, a thin, spectacled man named Carlos. "Whoever wrote that doesn't know Portuguese that well."

"What are you, a grammar teacher?" one of his comrades ribbed him.

"No, I'm serious," insisted Carlos. "Look, it says *no perigo*, not *em perigo*. No native Cabritan would talk like that. It's like it was written by a foreigner or something."

"That's what I thought, too," Bernardinho chimed in. "But I couldn't think of anybody who would do this. The only other American I know around here is you," he indicated Ray, "and you're his friend."

Ray's blood ran cold. The officers were looking at him oddly. Outwardly he worked hard to maintain his calm. He folded up the letter. "If you guys don't mind," he said casually, "I think I should take this. I'm going to be seeing *tenente* Diego this evening, and he will know what to do. Right now, I'm boiling in this heat and could really go for a cool beverage. Anybody for going to the *Macaco Verde*? First round's on me."

At the mention of free beer, the letter was forgotten, and a relieved Ray jumped into his taxi, clutching the incriminating letter in his hand.

Bernardinho watched them go, realizing too late that trusting the American taxi driver might have been a big mistake.

The crowd of Yamanis grew silent as Emídio Santana stepped into the circle. Max was suddenly aware of Santana's movements - light and catlike. His chest was muscular, his abdomen well-defined. Clearly, Santana was not someone to be taken lightly.

As Santana moved toward him he spoke low and in English, for Max's ears only.

"That was an entertaining display, *gringo*. But I am not a savage brute. I grew up in the rough-and-tumble brawls on the streets of Santo Expedito. When my father learned of my talent for fighting, he sent me to study under the best martial arts tutors in the world." He began to circle around Max, his eyes gleaming, his lip curled up in a snarl. "If I had to guess, I would say you were trained in the military. You may think you are something, but let me assure you, you are no match for me."

As Max watched his opponent carefully, he realized this was not swagger. Santana really believed every word he was saying.

"You will soon discover that your foot-soldier instruction was woefully insufficient for this fight, but by then it will be too late. For you see, I am going to kill you. You have been a thorn in my side long enough."

And with that, Santana lunged, and the next thing Max knew, he was lying on his back, gasping for air. Santana was standing over him.

"Get up, *gringo*," he snarled. "Your final lesson has just begun."

His mind racing, Max slowly stood to his feet and once again faced his opponent. He had never confronted anything like this. The goal of Santana's little speech had been to demoralize him, this he knew. But the move that the older man had just pulled proved beyond a shadow of a doubt that his opponent had superior fighting skills.

Better go on the offense. Can't give him a chance to do that to me again, Max thought. He immediately aimed a flying kick at Santana's face. Just as quickly, Santana grabbed Max's ankle and twisted it, throwing Max to the ground. Without hesitating, Max attacked again, this time from the ground, kicking wide in an attempt to knock his opponent over. Santana jumped up, avoiding it easily. In a flash Max was up. He came in low, fists pumping. He managed to deliver two solid blows to Santana's midsection, but these appeared to have no effect. Without flinching, Santana grabbed Max's arm and pulled him around, shoving him roughly to the ground. Once again Max rose, spitting dirt out of his mouth.

This guy is invincible! he thought, and as soon as he thought it, his mind flashed back to his training. "Nobody is invincible," he heard his instructor saying. "There is always a weak spot to be exploited."

Max faced his adversary once again. There was triumph in Santana's eyes. "You really don't know that much about me," he said softly, making a point to speak in Portuguese. "It's true, I was trained in the Army. But it wasn't infantry. I was a Green Beret. I have beaten Navy Seals in competitions and in bar fights. I have fought the Taliban, Columbian drug runners, and members of the Russian mob. I am still alive. Some of them aren't." Max was staring hard into Santana's eyes, looking for a sign of self-doubt. All he saw was scorn. Again the voice of his instructor:

"The most dangerous fighters are the ones devoid of emotion. If you can arouse any kind of emotion in your opponent, you have a much better chance of winning."

Santana's fist flashed out, catching Max on the chin. He flew backwards, landing once again in the dust, right in front of a horrified Ilana.

Ilana! The information Francesca had given him the other night in the alley came back to him. *Perhaps...*

As quick as Max could shake the clanging bells from his head, he staggered up and toward the triumphant Santana.

"You pack a good punch," he said, putting as much strength into his voice as possible. "But none of that will ever give you a chance with a girl like Ilana."

Was that a flicker he saw in Santana's eyes? Max pressed on. "Girls like her don't go for gigolos like you. You might beat me here, but you could never win someone like her." Red was creeping into Santana's face, starting at his neck and working its way up. "You see," Max continued, "a woman like Ilana deserves a man she can respect. And I don't think you can give her that. In fact, I bet the woman you are with now doesn't even..."

"Shut up!" screamed Santana as he lunged at Max. But this time Max was ready. He sidestepped smoothly and threw every ounce of energy he had into a roundhouse punch right to Santana's jaw. Jarring pain ran from Max's fist to his elbow, but Santana dropped like a rock.

So he can be hit, Max thought, and he felt a new confidence surge through his body. Santana leapt to his feet, and Max was on him again with a left, a right, and then a powerful kick to the middle. Santana tried to defend, but he was still in shock at what had just happened to him. Staggering back, a look of complete surprise on his face, Santana reached into his waistband.

Was it a knife or a gun? Max couldn't tell, but he wasn't taking any chances. He took a flying leap toward Santana and brought his foot around, delivering a wicked blow to the older man's cheek. Santana flew backwards, his body making a perfect arch in the air before landing in a heap. Several Yamani spectators had to scurry out of the way to avoid being hit.

"He killed Dr. Santana!" It was Diego, and his service revolver was drawn and pointed straight at Max. Max, breathing hard, turned toward him.

"Put that gun down!" It was the *presidente*. "Put it down, and that's an order!"

Diego lowered the weapon. Seeing Dr. Santana get thrashed by the American had fulfilled a secret fantasy of Osvaldo Ferraz. He might have to deal with the American later, but he would not let Diego kill him now. Besides, he was sure Santana was still alive - regrettably.

A crowd of people surrounded Santana, and presently Max saw him get up. Max was about to go over and talk to Ilana when a group of Yamani men surrounded him and, with a loud *whoop*, lifted him up onto their shoulders. As they ran victory laps around the clearing, Max could see Santana and his guests moving slowly toward their helicopter.

Emídio Santana was in a murderous mood. His humiliation at the hands of that *gringo* had removed all reason from his mind. As he watched Max being hoisted to the shoulders of the Yamani men and run around the village, his mind was completely possessed by thoughts of revenge.

Now he stood by the helicopter as his party prepared to leave. Max was amiably chatting with the men of the village, Ilana by his side, translating. What really burned at Santana's mind was not just that he had been beaten, but that the man who had beaten him had done it by calling out his feelings for the jungle beauty - the same girl who was now at *Max's* side. This was an altogether new feeling for Santana: that of wanting something but not being able to get it.

There was a light tap on his shoulder. Santana turned and saw Deigo.

"What is it?" Santana snapped in irritation.

"With all respect, sir," Diego said, "My grandmother on my father's side was a Yamani."

"What of it?" Santana asked. He was in no mood for stories.

"It's just that... well... I grew up listening to her tell me of the traditions of her people - the old traditions from before the white man came."

"And?"

"And," Diego took a deep breath. "And I think I have an idea you might like."

As the soldier laid forth his plan, a wicked smile crept across Dr. Santana's face.

Shadows gathered over the jungle clearing. The honored guests were preparing to go. The government helicopter, which was parked next to the FUNAPI chopper, was being warmed up.

In the trees just outside the clearing, Diego was conversing in hushed tones with Owanalahe, witch doctor of the Land-Dwellers.

"Esteemed Owanalahe, I bring you a message from your brother and friend, the great Santana."

Owanalahe grunted.

"We know how long you have chafed under certain... ah... regulations and restrictions imposed on you by the white man. Laws that forbid you to honor time-honored traditions."

Again, Owanalahe grunted. Diego continued.

"The great Santana has thought much about his brown brothers, and he is saddened by this great injustice that has been done by his ancestors. He wants me to tell you that, from now on, you may carry out your... ah... customs without fear of reprisal. You, as witch doctor, will doubtless be happy to hear that now you will be able to fully exercise your office."

There was no grunt, but the light in the man's beady eyes told Diego that his message was being received very well.

"And there is more. We have brought you two special gifts. One is the girl Ilana, who will make the perfect culmination to today's festival."

Again the grunt.

"The second is the white man who is with her. We are giving him to you as payment for the years that the white man has oppressed you."

Two grunts.

"Now, the great Santana will be displeased if he finds out that his gifts were not accepted."

There was a pause. Then the corpulent Owanalahe broke into a wide, tooth-deprived smile. "Tell the great Santana he should not worry," he said. "There will be much celebration tonight."

Diego's lips spread apart in a malicious smile. Then he turned and ran to the helicopter, whose blades were already turning slowly.

CHAPTER 18

TRADITIONAL VALUES

In the twelve hours he had spent in their midst Max had been truly fascinated by the Yamani people and their culture. Everything about them - the way they dressed in animal skins and feathers, the throbbing rhythm of their music, the whole-hearted way they threw themselves into their afternoon competitions - made Max wish he could learn more about them. So it was without hesitation that he accepted Ilana's invitation to spend the night with the tribe. "It will be fun," she had said. "Tomorrow I can show you more about life in the jungle."

After the presidential retinue had left, together with the helicopter that had brought Max that morning, Ilana had shown him to a hut where he would sleep. There was a mat in the corner, and Max placed his duffle bag at the head of it and lay down. Sleep was not long in coming. His dreams were full of gyrating natives, mixed with the faces of Emídio Santana, Diego, and President Ferraz. At one point he was surrounded by a group of Yamanis and he heard Ilana screaming in the background. He tried to get to her but the group of natives in front of him would not let him. The screams grew louder and more insistent.

"Max!!! Max!!!"

Suddenly Max sat bolt upright. Once again the sound of his name had awoken him.

"Max!!! Max!!!"

Jumping up he made for the doorway of the hut. Just as he reached it a group of warriors swarmed inside. He fought back tenaciously, but, outnumbered as he was, Max was overpowered in a matter of minutes. The natives dragged him outside, where a fearsome sight awaited him. A large stake was set up in the middle of the clearing, at about the spot where Ilana had done her dance that morning. Ilana herself was being dragged, kicking and screaming towards it. Her head dress was gone and her long black hair flew in all directions as she squirmed back and forth, trying to escape her captors. With admiration Max noted that a couple times she almost succeeded.

In front of the stake stood the corpulent native who Max had seen enter the forest with Diego earlier. His mind working frantically even as he was being dragged toward the stake, he put the pieces together. Somehow the Yamanis had been induced to kill them both.

Max and Ilana reached the wooden stake at the same time. The same strong cords were used to bind them both to it, back to back. Ilana was yelling and cursing something in the native tongue. Max couldn't imagine that it was pretty.

All three tribes were present for the event. The drums started their hypnotic rhythms, and the warriors began a lurid dance around the two victims.

"Care to fill me in?" he asked, more in an attempt to calm her down than anything else.

"Somebody told them that they needed to revive an old custom, and we are to be its first victims."

"What old custom is that?"

Ilana briefly strained against the ropes, then answered. "Before the Portuguese came the Yamanis used to sacrifice a young girl at each celebration. In that way they thought to perpetuate the sacrifice of Ilanamihi."

"A young girl, huh. That explains why you're here, but what about me? Why am I included in this year's festivities?"

"They said that the white men told them you were a gift to them...something about making amends for years of oppression."

"And they told you this?" Max asked.

Ilana sighed. "At first they had the notion that I would be OK with the plan. They explained the whole thing to me - how the white men said they should return to their old customs, how we were gifts from the white men to them, how the white men would be offended if these gifts were not promptly...accepted. When I was less than cooperative they took me by force."

"And what is to be the mode of execution?" Max wondered.

"See those six spears stuck in the ground over there?"

"Yes."

"Three for me, three for you."

"So, is this one of the traditions we should be set on preserving? Your call."

"This is not the time for sarcasm, Max." It was the first time she had ever spoken sharply to him. Under the circumstances, Max couldn't exactly blame her. She began straining hopelessly at the ropes again.

"I wouldn't do that if I were you." Max advised.

"Why not?"

"You should save your energy."

"What?"

Max did not answer. His mind was actively examining the situation from all angles. The corpulent shaman stood in front of the stake. In front of him the six spears stuck in the ground. Beyond them, the Yamani danced in an ever tightening circle.

Those spears are very, very close...

"Ilana," Max said in as low a voice as he could manage and still be heard. "Listen to me very carefully. As soon as you feel the ropes fall I want you to grab one of those spears and hold it right to the fat guy's neck."

"But the ropes..."

"Just trust me. Are you ready?"

"I'm ready."

"Ok, suck in your breath."

Ilana obeyed, and Max relaxed his chest, arm, and leg muscles which he had flexed while being tied to the stake. To Ilana's surprise the ropes fell to the ground around her ankles.

In a flash Max had jumped on the shaman, grabbing the fat man's neck with one hand and twisting his arm behind him with another. Almost as quickly Ilana grabbed one of the spears and held the point of it to the rubbery folds of the shaman's neck.

Immediately the dancing stopped. Where one second there had been the cacophony of drums and shouting, the next you could have heard a feather drop. Max knew that this moment was vital.

"Tell them to let us through." Max ordered, and Ilana translated. Seeing how the shaman's eyes widened in fear as she spoke Max was sure she added a couple imprecations of her own to the command. The man cried out, and the warriors in front of him stepped aside. Like the parting of the Red Sea, a path opened up for Max, Ilana, and their quivering captive. As a precaution he released his grip on the shaman's neck long enough to grab another spear as they entered the passageway.

Max could feel the host of dark eyes on them as they walked between the columns of hostile warriors. He knew he had to keep the mob off their guard - keep control of the situation. He was remembering his reading in the little used bookstore which had told of how the Yamani are utterly dependent on their shamans for protection from a veritable all-you-can-eat buffet of evil spirits. Max hoped against hope that this century-old report was still true.

He spoke softly to Ilana. "Tell them that if they take one step we will skewer their beloved Shaman like a wild boar." Ilana smiled at the imagery and repeated his threat. The warriors closest to them stepped back, widening the path they were following.

After what seemed like an eternity they reached the end of the human corridor. Before them was the black jungle. Behind them, several hundred angry warriors.

The jungle it was.

Still holding the hapless shaman they plunged into the under-brush. Ilana took charge. "Follow me."

Pushing the shaman as quickly as he could Max did his best to keep up with the lithe woman in front of him. Clearly she was in her natural habitat and, although he had been through extensive jungle training as a Green Beret, she was easily outpacing him.

After half an hour of slashing through the dense underbrush they came to a small creek. Ilana stopped.

"We should leave him here. We will make better time without him." Max agreed and released his grip on the shaman, but not before removing a knife from the native's waste-band. "I think I'll keep this."

Ilana spoke to him rapidly in the Yamani tongue, and he scam-pered away into the darkness. For his size, Max observed, he was remarkably nimble.

"What did you tell him?"

"That if he knows what is good for him he will tell the warriors not to follow us."

"Do you think it will work?"

"Not a chance."

As if give credence to her prediction drums started beating om-inously in the distance.

"Those are the war drums," she said. "Quickly, follow me." With that she jumped into the shallow creek and began to wade up-stream. Having no other option, Max followed suit.

At his decrepit farm house Ray, lost in his thoughts, all but ig-nored the beer in front of him. His deal with Santana had involved him in some pretty shady activities on more than one occasion. It had been so long that his conscience had long-since stopped bothering him.

Until now. Suddenly he was plagued with feelings he had not known since...well, it had been a very long time. As if watching a grainy home movie, he could see himself at this very table several weeks ago, cutting out letters from a magazine and then gluing them carefully onto a piece of paper. When he was finished he held the paper up and examined his work.

Mr. and Mrs. Blake: Enjoy your children while you can. After Monday you will not see them again.

It was a cowardly trick for Santana to pull, and Ray had no idea why he was doing it. Actually, Santana had not done it. He had. Acting on orders from Diego he had manufactured the note, put it in a Manila envelope, and then placed it under the door of the Blake's home.

He had tried every which way to rationalized his actions. I'm really doing them a favor. They should never have come here. They have no idea what they are up against.

But the thought came back to him with increasing force: *I threatened children!!!* Ray tried hard not to think of what might have happened had the Blakes opted not to leave. What would he have been required to do then?

Not surprisingly, the Blakes had called *him* to take them to the airport, trusting as they were of a fellow American, and completely unsuspecting of his role in the affair. That is when things had taken an unexpected turn with the arrival of Max the very moment they were leaving. Now the situation was completely out of hand. Max had no children, and was completely immune to any kind of intimidation. In fact, intimidation seemed to make him dig in his heels and fight harder. And what was worse, *she* was involved. The very person he had been trying to protect all these years was now in the center ring of this three-ring circus.

Ray lifted his fist with the intention of banging it on the table in frustration - and then stopped, fist in mid-air. His keen ears had heard the sound of footsteps outside. He listened carefully.

Nothing.

Not trusting the silence he slowly reached down and withdrew his .45 from its hiding place in his waistband. Pointing it at the door in front of him he turned off the safety.

"I heard that." The voice outside the door was Diego's. "The hospitality of this place gets worse every time I stop by."

Swearing softly to himself Ray placed his gun on the table. "Come on in," he said, not at all enthusiastically.

The door opened and in stepped the soldier. He was pristinely dressed, and he carried himself in a haughty manner that made the old American soldier want to take a swing at him.

If only my old Ranger buddies could see me now, Ray thought as Diego stepped smartly across the room. Taking orders from this clown. You've come a long way, Ray ol' boy.

Diego stood before him, as if waiting for an invitation to sit. One never came.

"I bring good news," he said finally, an ironic smile playing around his thin lips. It was the only kind of smile that ever appeared there.

"Lay it on me," said Ray.

"The situation with the nosy *americano* has been cared for."

"Really?" The affirmation caught Ray off guard. "So soon?"

"Oh indeed. We were presented with an unexpected opportunity and we took advantage of it. He will not be bothering us anymore. In fact, he will not be bothering anybody anymore."

Ray understood the implications of that last statement, and he found it difficult to conceal his surprise.

"Really? I thought the old boy would give you more trouble than that."

"And what gave you that impression?"

Ray thought back to the things he had observed...things he had left out of his reports to Diego and Company.

"Oh...nothing. Just a hunch I had. So how'd you get him? Mugging gone horribly wrong? Freak auto accident? Unexplained suicide?"

"Oh no, no." Diego was actually gloating. "Much more creative than that. He was attacked by ferocious tribe of Yamani Indians, hungry for human sacrifice. In fact, at this very moment he is most likely attending what you Americans call a 'barbecue' - as the main course."

Poor devil, Ray though. Bet he put up a good fight, though.

"So this means that I am off that job?"

"Oh indeed. Here is your payment. The government of Cabrito is grateful." With that Diego threw a wad of cash on the table. Absently Ray picked it up and thumbed through the bills. Diego continued. "You may consider this your last payment from us."

Ray looked up quizzically.

"We are aware that your service to us has been contingent on our protection of a certain young lady, one Ilana - up until recently the head of FUNAPI."

Ray tensed. "What do you mean 'up until recently'?"

"Unfortunately the *senhorita* Ilana was, shall we say, collateral damage in our most recent operation. She has suffered the same fate as the *americano.*"

"What?!?" An overwhelming rage overtook the older man and he stood up and grabbed his pistol. Diego never lost his cool.

"It is a pity. She was certainly a lovely morsel. I am sure the natives have found her a tasty one."

He chuckled at his own cleverness. Then he turned his back on the enraged American and stalked from the room. Ray, shaking with helpless grief and anger, watched him go. He never knew what kept him from putting a bullet through Diego at that moment. Slowly he sank back into the chair, put his head on the table and wept, his large frame shaking violently in uncontrollable sobs.

Diego walked down the path toward the gate, where he had left Cascavel with his car. Though his steps were measured and outwardly he was cool and collected, inwardly he was elated.

Ever since he had begun working as a special agent of the *presidente* - and subsequently for Dr. Santana - he had grown to despise the old American. He regarded him as a necessary evil, someone to be tolerated. But he despised him. His alcoholism, his poor living habits, his casual demeanor, his lack of proper respect for authority - all of these things grated on Diego's high opinion of Diego.

If Diego were to be completely honest with himself he would have to admit that, deep down, he also feared the older American. There was no doubt that, though much older than he, Raymond Sand could clean Diego's clock in anything close to a fair fight. And there was something Diego saw in Ray's eyes every time they talked that let the young soldier know he would enjoy the opportunity.

Now Ray would be out of his hair. For good. True, on some level it was a shame to lose such a good agent. Ray had the American "can-do" attitude that made him especially valuable. And his motivation - the protection of the Yamani girl - guaranteed that he was fully cooperative.

But there would be other people to subvert, other stooges who could serve Diego's interests just as well. And it had given Diego a special pleasure to see Raymond Sand completely destroyed in front of him, without his having to lift a finger.

Cascavel was waiting for him at the end of the grassy driveway. *Speaking of stooges...*

"Did everything go as planned?"

"Quite," said Diego with a thin smile. Cascavel held the car door for him as he slipped into the driver's seat. Then he turned to his new lackey.

"You stay here. The minute the *americano* steps out of his house, shoot him."

Morning arrived and the sunlight streamed through the openings in the dense jungle canopy. The effect was not unlike that caused by the morning sun as it shown through the stain glass windows of the little country church in rural New York, but that was the farthest thing from Max's mind as he ran pell-mell across the jungle floor, following his more nimble Indian guide. Max knew they were heading steadily north, but other than that he knew nothing of their destination. It was best just to trust the figure running tirelessly in front of him. Suddenly a large rock cliff loomed in front of them. Ilana stopped and turned to him.

"We are going to have to climb," she said. "On the other side is a wide valley with a river that runs down from the mountain. The stream we crossed earlier is one of its tributaries. We can follow it to the ocean. Then it is a short trip up the coast to the nearest town."

"Why didn't we just follow the tributary when we crossed it?" Max wanted to know.

"Because it would have taken us through a couple of Yamani villages before we arrived. I didn't figure you would be thrilled with that idea."

"Sorry for asking," said Max. "Lead on."

Max was an experienced climber, but once again the jungle-bred girl outpaced him. When he arrived, huffing and puffing, at the top of the cliff he found Ilana staring into the distance. Following her gaze, Max's jaw dropped open.

"This has changed a lot from when I was a little girl," Ilana whispered.

Above them and to the northeast the *Dedo de Deus* mountain rose in green majesty. Before them stretched the river valley. From their perch Max could see where, in the distance, the river emptied into the sea.

But the Ilana was paying no attention to the natural contours. Instead she was staring at a fully operational plantation directly in front of them. Max knew immediately what he was looking at. As a Green Beret he had helped to destroy a couple of identical plantations in Columbia.

The jungle was cleared for several acres on either side of the river, and row upon row of a lush, green coca plants grew in its place. At the center there was a group of low buildings: barracks, an administration building, and what appeared to be a laboratory.

"A facility for the processing and shipping of cocaine." Max quoted from the official order he had been given prior to his Columbia mission. "Look at the trucks—isn't that the symbol of the Cabritan army?"

Ilana nodded, speechless with anger.

"I am going to hazard a guess," Max continued, "that we have discovered the *real* reason Santana didn't want anybody nosing around Yamani territory."

"And it would appear they have help," added Ilana between clenched teeth. She pointed to a pile of large cargo containers stacked by the river. Max followed her gesture, and then gasped in disbelief. On them was clearly painted with the logo of Sherman Pharmaceutical Group, Incorporated.

"Max," Ilana asked. "Didn't you say your last name is Sherman."

Max groaned inwardly. He had known this would come up eventually. He was sure—no, he was absolutely certain—that SPGI had nothing to do with the scene before them. Yet, how to explain all the complications...

"Ilana, if we get out of this I will explain everything to you. But for now, think of this: if I had anything to do with that outfit I would not be running from a group of wild sav...indiginous people right now."

Ilana was pondering his response when the sound of drums - considerably closer than before - came to their ears. Max was almost grateful for the interruption.

"We obviously can't go to the river," Ilana mused. "The people there will not be happy to see us. We can't go downstream because we will run into the Yamani coming this way. That means we have to go east and try to double back that way, and hope there are no Yamani coming from that direction. Let's go!"

CHAPTER 19

HIDDEN TALENTS

James Madison Rockwell knew he needed to act, and *fast*. He had left the Yamani celebration in the same helicopter with the other guests, noticing as he did so that Max had stayed behind. This in itself was not surprising to him. After all, this was Maxwell Sherman, and there was a beautiful girl involved. Unaware of the depth of Max's recent spiritual transformation, he assumed that Max was simply following up on his latest conquest. No surprises there.

But in the helicopter on the way home Dr. Santana and his companions - James was under no delusion as to where the real power lay on the island - had talked freely among themselves. And in doing so they made a grave mistake.

One of the qualities that made Mr. Rockwell so effective in the service of SPGI was his thoroughness in every aspect of his work. This included learning the language of the countries where he was stationed. Mr. Rockwell had racked up an impressive list of languages in his repertoire. Among these (thanks to a stint in Brazil) was Portuguese. Though he usually had a command of the language by the time he arrived in a determined country, he never let on - allowing the nationals fit him into their pre-conceived mold of the ignorant American. Thus he was privy to conversations that were not intended for his ears.

As the elated officials and unsavory soldier gleefully celebrated the demise of the Maxwell Sherman, James Rockwell listened with growing horror. With herculean effort he remain stone-faced all the way to the airport, and then in the limo from the airport to the hotel. As soon as he entered his room he reached for the phone. Then, thinking better of it, he opened his drawer and pulled out the satellite phone. Quickly punching in the familiar number, he waited until he heard the answer on the other end.

"Hello James. What is it?"

"Ma'am, I think you need to get to Cabrito right away."

"Why?"

"It's Maxwell."

There was a pause at the other end of the line.

"I'll be there."

Mr. Rockwell sat on his bed. A feeling of helplessness overwhelmed him. There was absolutely nothing he could do - an uncomfortable realization for someone so used to being in control. There was nowhere he could turn...nothing he could do...*wait!*

"The note!" he said to nobody in particular. His mind went back to the banquet at the *Casa Branca*, and how the exquisitely beautiful and yet terribly unhappy wife of Dr. Santana had stared at him throughout the evening. It made him curious, because while he was quite a talented businessman, he was short and balding - not the type of man supermodels generally found interesting.

But as Dr. Santana and his wife were leaving the woman had dropped a business card on his plate, then exited without looking at him. Picking it up, James saw that there was writing on the back. It was in Portuguese:

I am Francesca. I remember you from a fashion show in Rio, and I know you speak Portuguese. Things here are not what they seem. Only call this number if you need help.

It was a straw, but James Madison Rockwell grasped it firmly. Retrieving the card from his wallet he picked up his satellite phone and punched in the number.

Emídio Santana loved his yacht, and therefore his wife hated it with a passion. She spent most of her time in the old Santana family estate - which for the most part kept her away from the man she loathed.

Right now she paced the floor of the spacious parlour. Since the call from Mr. Rockwell earlier in the day, she had been worried sick about the fate of the young American missionary. She had told the SPGI agent what she knew - which was considerable. Now, as dawn was breaking, she hoped against hope that Max had been able to survive the night.

If he has not, if anything has happened to him... Her mind filled with scorn for her husband and his lackeys. *If something has happened to him, they will pay.*

She rang for Itamar and Inácio, her only real friends in the world. They had been with her during her entire career, and had continued in her employ after her marriage to Dr. Santana.

The two men entered the room.

"Boys, the *missionário americano* is in danger. I need information, and the one who has it is that *taxista* Raymond Sand. Go pay him a visit."

"Right away, *senhora* Francesca," Itamar said.

"Yes, right away," echoed his brother Inácio.

The two left the room, leaving Francesca alone to fret about the safety of the American missionary. Her mind went back to that other missionary, the one who had come to her small town in Brazil so many years before. She remembered him as a man of prayer. When he prayed, even with his deplorable Portuguese, she got the feeling that he had ushered the entire congregation into the presence of God.

Pray. That's all I can do now.

Slowly she kicked off her high-heels and sank to the floor. "God," she began, "it's been a long time. I've made a lot of stupid decisions since we last talked. But this isn't about me. It's about one of your servants, and he needs your help right now."

The noonday sun was high in the sky, and although the two fugitives could not see it through the canopy of trees, they could certainly feel its effects as the rainforest became an oven.

They had kept a fairly even pace since that morning, but no matter how hard or in which direction they ran, Ilana and Max could hear the war drums getting louder. Max could tell that panic was starting to take hold of his companion.

"They're coming from the south and the west. If they are successful in cutting us off from the east, we're finished," she said between breaths as they paused for a rest. Max, leaning on a tree-trunk and trying to get his breathing back to normal, knew she was right.

"If you have any clout with your God, now would be the time to cash in," she said.

Despite the circumstances Max chuckled. "It's impossible to have clout with the God of the universe," he said. "Heaven doesn't work like a government agency."

"I can't believe you're correcting my theology at a time like this!" she said, with an ever-so-small hint of playfulness to her voice. "What we could really use is some way to call and get help, because we are not going to be able to outrun all of them."

They began to run again, this time heading north. Max looked heavenward. "Lord, you heard her. Neither one of us can really demand anything of you..."

"Get to the point!!!" Ilana hissed.

"...but we could really use some help about now. We don't know your plans, but from our perspective things look pretty bleak." Then, as a post-script, "One more thing, Lord, Ilana here really doesn't believe in you, and is in no way ready to meet you. It would be wonderful if you could show her just a little glimpse of your power right about now."

"Well that was sweet," said Ilana. "But, unless we find a pay phone out here somewhere, we are...as you Americans say...up the creek."

No sooner had she made this comment than they ran into a small clearing, and both of them stopped dead in their tracks, mouths agape. There before them, outlined in a single ray of sun that descended from an opening in the jungle canopy above, was a pay phone. Stenciled on the side of the faded-blue covering were the words "*Alô-Cabrito, Adm. F. Rabelo*".

Ilana looked at Max. "No way!"

Max just shrugged in wonder. Slowly they approached it. Max cleared a couple vines and cobwebs from the front of the protective covering and lifted the receiver from the metal hook. He put it to his ear and then, slowly, put it to Ilana's ear. Her eyes widened.

There was a dial tone!

"But wait, how do we call?" she asked. "It's a pay phone. It requires tokens. And even if we had tokens, this is one of the old pay phones. Today's tokens wouldn't fit in it...what are you looking at Max?"

Max was staring at the necklace that Ilana had been wearing since yesterday. It consisted of a string decorated with bones, beads and other assorted trinkets. Max was especially interested in the trinket right in the middle. He reached out his hand and lifted the necklace to inspect it.

"What's this?" he asked.

"Is this really the time to be..."

With a swift motion Max yanked it from her neck.

"Hey! That is a tribal good luck charm."

Max looked up at her. "Under the circumstances, I don't think your tribe will mind." He held up the trinket that had caught his attention. It looked like a coin, except that it's surface was serrated. On the front were engraved the words "*Alô Cabrito*".

"Officer, I'd like to make that phone call now."

Ilana was dumbstruck. "You mean I have been wearing a phone token this whole time?" Then the drums in the distance brought her back to their present situation.

"Quick, who do we call? Everybody I can think of is with the government...probably not a good idea right now."

"I have just the person," Max said after a moment's thought. He reached for his wallet, and, opening it, removed the business card that read "Transporte Raimundo". "If anybody has the resources to get us out of here, it will be good ol' Ray," he declared with confidence. "Here goes!"

With that he dropped the coin in the slot and dialed the number.

"It's ringing!" he said, excitedly. Then, after a few moments. "It's still ringing." The phone continued to ring and ring, until finally it cut out and, with horror, Ilana and Max heard the token drop into the bowels of the phone. The incessant drumming sounded louder in their ears. Frustrated, Max hung up the phone slowly and turned to Ilana.

"We should start running." he said.

"Yes we should." she replied softly. "But we need to run north, because the drums are now coming from the south, the east, and the west. They have cut us off."

Ray was at his house, still with his head on the table. Scattered around him were scores of empty beer bottles. After hearing what

Diego had told him he had given himself completely to his faithful companion. Now, in his sleep, he was back in Viet Nam. The bells were ringing and calling him to action. He searched frantically for his equipment, with no success. The bells rang louder and more urgently, two-short bursts at a time.

Ring-ring.

Ring-ring.

Ring-ring.

That was strange. The alarm never sounded that way in 'Nam. That ring sounded more like...

Suddenly Ray was awake. The phone was ringing.

Ring-ring.

Ring-ring.

Ray grabbed the receiver and held it to his ear. Dial tone.

"Oh well," he muttered to himself as he began to clear the bottles off his table. "Whoever it is will call back."

Then he stopped . *That ring!*

That was the distinctive ring of the *Alô Cabrito* telephone system. He should know, because he had helped to install it. The only problem was, all of those phones had long since been disconnected. All but one...

Suddenly alert, Ray's brain began to function at full tilt.

Why would anybody be calling me from the jungle phone? There was only one logical reason. Somehow Max had gotten himself out of that jam and had stumbled on the pay phone. And if Max got away, *Ilana might be with him!*

Ray ran his fingers through his thick shock of grey hair. *I know exactly where that phone is. I just have to get there quick. And that won't be a problem.* He started toward the front door, slipping his Colt .45 into his belt as he did.

Nope, back door will be quicker. Also...better visit the arsenal. Almost at a run Ray descended the stairway to his basement.

Ever since beginning his current line of work Ray had prepared for the day in which his home might have to become a fortress. He was quite confident that the time would come when his benefactors would turn against him, and he wanted to be ready. Fortunately, his work afforded him contact with all sorts of shady characters, including arms dealers.

Opening a heavy wooden door in the stone wall, he turned on the light and scanned his private collection of armaments. Nobody, not even Diego - or *especially not Diego* - knew about this room. He grabbed a couple pistols and several rounds of ammunition for each. Then he pulled two M16s off the wall and strapped them to his back. Finally, he picked up a gunny sack full of hand grenades.

After slinging on several ammunition belts he went upstairs and raced out the back door to his barn, on the way grabbing a length of sturdy rope and slinging it over his shoulders.

Opening the door he ran down the center aisle, passing by the VW, the Mercedes, the '57 Chevy, all the way to the back where his *magnum opus* sat covered with a tarp. Ray opened the large double doors at the back of the barn, then turned and, with one swift motion, removed the covering.

CHAPTER 20

MISSIONARY AVIATION

His continual quest for junk cars to fix up led Ray to an abandoned air base one day. It had been used by the RAF during World War II as a fueling stop between their Caribbean colonies and the African front. Opening a rusty hangar, he had found the Hawker Hart Demon sitting there just as it had been left decades earlier.

The Hawker Hart was an airplane whose time never came. A sturdy bi-plane built by Great Britain between the Wars, it came in both fighter and bomber versions. By the opening of hostilities, however, it was hopelessly obsolete - no match for the Japanese Zeros or German Messerschmits. Still, the hardy planes were put to use in behind-the-lines operations, and in the defense of places that had little chance of being attacked.

Made out of metal - not the flimsy canvas of World War I-era planes - the two-seater Hawker Hart was different in other ways as well. Its nose came to a sharp point, and in contrast to the usual arrangement, the pilot sat in the front while the passenger sat in back. The passenger seat was also equipped with an air-cooled machine-gun, giving the plane a sting as well as a bite.

After sneaking it out of the hangar late at night Ray had parked it in his barn. His other projects then fell by the wayside as he concentrated his energies on the plane. Once it was fixed he cleared out a small runway behind the barn took it on a maiden flight. Though his military pilot's license had long expired, the controls felt natural in his hand. The thrill of flying was eclipsed by one other thought: he now had a way to get off the island should the need arise - and, as the Demon was a two-seater—he could take a passenger.

Finding ammunition for the guns had been a challenge, but contacts in the underworld had come through for him. Now, with steady hands, he threaded the rounds of long, pointed bullets into the two front machine guns. Then he went to the back and did the same with the tail gun.

Finishing this task he removed the blocks from the wheels and pulled the aircraft out from the barn.

Once outside, Ray stashed his weapons in the front cockpit. Taking the length of rope from his shoulder he tied a rock to one end, and the other end he fastened to the cockpit seat.

Once he was finished he went to the front of the plane and spun the propeller.

"Contact!"

Determined not to fail his new benefactor a second time, Cascavel kept watch at Ray's house all night long with the sights of the shiny new rifle Diego had given him trained at the door. As morning turned into day, and there was no sign of his target, sleepiness took hold of him, and, after a brief struggle, Cascavel dozed off.

He was awakened by the roar of an engine. He looked up just in time to see the biplane roar overhead. Blinking in the sunlight, he watched as it made a wide turn toward the jungle. As the aircraft banked Cascavel made out the figure of Raymond Sand, his supposed target, sitting in the pilot's seat. He was about to grab his gun and try to fire a couple shots at the disappearing plane when he got his second shock of the day.

Two very large men stood in front of him. Both of them held machine guns pointed straight at his heart.

"Make a move for that gun and you will die, *amigo*," said Inácio.

"Right. You'll die," echoed Itamar.

Slowly, Cascavel lifted his hands into the air.

Max and Ilana ran for their lives. Adrenaline coursed through their bodies and they flew through the jungle as if they had spent the night in restful sleep.

And still the pounding of the drums grew closer. It was behind them, on either side of them, and - as Ilana now realized - in front of them. They were completely surrounded.

God!!! she screamed in her mind. She would surely have screamed out loud if the burning in her lungs were not so great. *I don't know if you are there. I have not paid much attention to you in my life. But if you can bring it upon yourself to pay attention to us now...HELP!!!*

Suddenly they broke into a large, grassy clearing. Doubtless it had at one time been a Yamani village. Now it was a big field the jungle had yet to reclaim. As they ran across the grass Ilana looked behind her, and saw a line of warriors emerge from the trees.

"You run!" shouted Max. "I'll hold them off here for as long as I can."

"It's no use!" exclaimed Ilana with what sounded like a sob. Max turned, and saw warriors emerging from the trees behind them. "We're surrounded."

Max turned to Ilana and embraced her. "Ilana," he shouted above the noise of the drums. "Ilana, trust Jesus!"

Ilana closed her eyes and held on tightly to Max. He was so strong, so calm in the face of certain death. Whatever it was he had, she wanted it, whatever, *whoever* it was he was trusting, she wanted to trust him, too.

Jesus, I have no idea who you are. But Max trusts you, and I trust you, too. I trust nothing else...just you. And, it would seem I am going to be meeting you soon.

A calm washed over her, a calm she had never known, even when she was not surrounded by angry natives intent on her destruction. It was a serene feeling, not that everything would be alright, but that everything *was* alright.

"Thank you, Jesus," she whispered. Eyes still closed, Ilana awaited the spears.

Instead, another sound began to overtake the sound of the drums. It sounded like...propellers?

She opened her eyes. The warriors were still there, just a few yards away, but they were not looking at Max and Ilana. Instead, their faces were lifted upward. Ilana followed their gaze, and, to her amazement, saw a silver-colored biplane in full dive, coming straight at them.

Just as it looked as if the plane would surely crash it pulled up, and at the same time fire sprouted from either side of its nose.

Rat-a-tat-TAT.

Rat-a-tat-TAT.

The ground boiled in front of a section of the warriors and they stumbled for cover. The other warriors stepped back, their faces showing panic. The plane zoomed over head, and then climbed straight up into the air. It executed a perfect loop and dove once again.

Rat-a-tat-TAT.

Rat-a-tat-TAT.

This time another section of warriors dove for cover. Many of the others were already running away. As the plane roared overhead Max was able to identify the pilot.

"Ray!"

Ilana was incredulous. "How did he know..?"

"Not the most important question right now," Max observed. He was watching Ray. As the plane approached for the third time Max saw the rope drop from the cockpit.

"Ilana, hang on to me to me tightly, like you have never hung on to anything in your life."

The Indian girl did not need to be told twice. She enveloped Max with her arms and legs. Max braced himself as the plane approached. The dangling rope came closer...closer...

Max leapt into the air and caught the rope with his hands. The pull - exacerbated by Ilana's extra weight - almost yanked his arms out of their sockets. But he held on, and in the blink of an eye they were swinging high over the jungle, leaving behind several hundred stunned Yamanis.

"Yaaaaaaaaaaaaaaaaaaaaaaaaaaaaaarrrrrrrrrrrgh!"

Slowly, hand over hand, muscles bulging with the effort, Max pulled himself and Ilana upward. In the cockpit Ray struggled to steady the plane while Max climbed. Finally Max's hands appeared on the edge, and then his head. He smiled.

"I didn't know *Transporte Raimundo* included air service."

"It does, but it'll cost ya extra. You sure do get yourself into some scrapes."

With great effort Max pulled himself the rest of the way onto the biplane and swung Ilana into the back seat facing backwards.

"Where are you going to sit?" asked Ilana.

"No room for me in there. Ray, hand me the rope."

Rope in hand, Max pulled himself onto the top wing. Then he looped the rope around, securing his waist to the wing.

"Time to head home!" Ray hollered above the din of the propellers.

Peering down into the cockpit, Max saw the small arsenal Ray had brought along with him. He had an idea.

"Hey Ray, you up for a detour?"

Emídio Santana smiled in satisfaction as he looked at the large, rust-colored sea-containers marked *Sherman Pharmaceutical Group, Incorporated*. He walked, flanked by one of his lieutenants, through the camp that comprised the base of operations of his pet project: *Operation Snow Storm*.

For years Emídio had lived under the shadow of his billionaire (some said trillionaire, nobody really knew for sure) father, George Santana. The *scion* administered the family's holdings in Cabrito - which was pretty much the entire island of Cabrito - while the patriarch manipulated the world markets. Everything Emídio did was part of his father's grand scheme.

This project was also part of the elder Santana's grand scheme, with one notable difference: the idea had originated with the son. With pride Emídio recalled the meeting in which he had presented his idea: use the fertile valley of the Ipuna river on Cabrito - virtually unknown in the international community - as a source for the production of narcotics for the US and the entire Western world.

Drugs had long been part of the elder Santana's *modus operandi*. His money supported the manufacturing and shipping processes while his political action groups in the US and Europe lobbied for weaker law enforcement and legalization.

Manufacturing had always been the weakest link. Host countries, no matter how unstable, had a nasty habit of getting a conscience and making things difficult for the growers and processors - in many cases with the help of the US military.

Here on Cabrito, however, things could be different. He owned these islands. The river valley was fertile and hidden. And, with the arrival of SPGI, they had the perfect cover for exportation. Why, even now the first batch of sea containers filled with fully processed cocain were waiting for the barges that would take them to sea. As his family owned all the major shipping concerns here - as well as all of the inspection agents - every container would be completely legit. Upon arrival the "hot" containers would be diverted to people pre-prepared to receive them, and their contents distributed to a ravenous consumer base. Soon every American city would be high with drugs grown and processed right here on Cabrito. And the proceeds would fill the offshore accounts of the Santana family.

Emídio's eyes went from the fields of cocoa to the storage bins and processing labs. Yes, his father would be proud of him. Emídio would be very careful to recount in full detail how he had ruthlessly removed every obstacle in his path. He had nursed this project from the very beginning when, years before, he had nipped the *Alô Cabrito* program in the bud because of its sudden incursion into the jungle, dangerously close to the intended area of operations. To do that it had been necessary to remove that clown Rabelo from office and replace him with someone much more...pliable. Osvaldo Ferraz had been just the man: easy to manipulate, and even easier to intimidate.

The missionaries, with their constant poking around in the jungle and romantic notion of evangelizing the Yamanis, had been a particularly persistent headache. It seemed that as soon as one left, another arrived, burning with passion for the "poor, unreached natives". Yet he had managed to convince all of them, in one way or another, that it was not worth the risk. Only this Maxwell fellow refused to be intimidated. Emídio took the sound of drums he was hearing from the jungle that morning as a sign that the young American had ceased to be a threat. He and Ilana were now sacrifices to some minor Yamani deity.

The thought of Ilana's demise made him smile. What had been ardent passion for her had given way easily to burning hate once her rejection of him had become plain. Nobody...*nobody* said no to Emídio Santana.

More precisely, nobody says no to me and lives to tell about it, he thought with no small degree of satisfaction.

The distant sound of a motor interrupted his happy thoughts. Annoyed, he turned to see why his pilot was starting the helicopter so soon. But the helicopter sat on its pad, blades at rest. Then he realized that the sound was coming from the air.

Looking up he saw a biplane approaching. "Who is authorized to arrive at this hour?" he demanded of the commander of the military unit guarding the plant.

"Nobody, sir," the man replied. He lifted a pair of binoculars to his eyes. "That plane is not connected to this project."

Emídio grabbed the binoculars and looked through them. What he saw made his blood run cold. In the cockpit was Ray, the old American.

"Diego was supposed to eliminate him," he muttered. Then his jaw dropped in shock. In the back seat was Ilana! How could that be? He adjusted his binoculars and looked again. It was her alright - and very much alive.

Then he saw Max, lashed in a prone position to the top wing, right above the cockpit. And Max was looking down the sights of an M16.

"Battle positions!!!! We are under attack!"

Emídio's frantic screams were too late. Already the front guns of the ancient plane were coughing flame. The target, Emídio's helicopter, was instantly riddled with holes. One of the bullets struck the gas tank, and a giant ball of fire erupted, leaving a twisted, smoking wreckage where the helicopter once sat.

The aircraft swung down almost in front of Emídio, and he could see that Max's M16 was also firing, with devastating results.

Max was as comfortable holding an M16 as a mother is holding her child. Even with his unorthodox firing position the bullets did his bidding, smashing the windows of the drug lab, and destroying the equipment inside. Emídio watched helplessly as the tires on the troop transport trucks deflated, one after another.

From his perch on top of the plane Max eyed the destruction with satisfaction as the plane rose from its dive.

"You fire that thing like you've done once or twice it before," Ray hollered up to Max.

"A couple times. I was a Green Beret."

"I knew it!" Ray yelled. "The way you took out that *bandido* a few weeks back, I knew there was more to you than people thought."

"You saw that?"

"Yep. Knew you were military, shoulda guessed you were a fellow Beret."

"Fellow Beret? You mean you were special forces too?"

"Five years in 'Nam. You?"

"Iraq, Afghanistan, and a couple other places."

"I hate to break up this veteran's reunion," said Ilana from the back seat, "but I think we have more pressing matters."

"She's right," said Ray. "Are you ready for another run?"

"Lock and load!" shouted Max. At this Ray executed a flip and turn which gave Max a whole new understanding of the old man's taxi-driving technique - and almost made him vomit.

On the ground Emídio Santana had managed to gather a few soldiers around him and was trying to organize a defense. As the plane approached a second time he directed the men. "Aim carefully, gentlemen. That plane is fragile. We should be able to bring it down easily."

As soon as the words left his mouth something fell from the plane and landed on the ground in front of them. It was a grenade.

"Dive for cover!" he shouted - needlessly, it turned out, as the men were doing just that. As he jumped away the force from the explosion propelled him forward onto his face. Scrambling to his knees he watched in horror as grenade after grenade fell with accuracy. One by one buildings went up in flames: the storage facilities, the residential barracks, the barges waiting in the river.

"Yeeeehaaaaa!" A cry of jubilation escaped Ray's throat.

"Boo Yah!" echoed Max.

Apparently, Green Berets have their own language, Ilana mused.

"Ready for one more?" asked Ray.

"Hammer time!" yelled Max. "Hand me up that other M16."

"What's our target?" Ray shouted as he maneuvered the plane into position.

"Pretty much the only thing left standing!" Max shouted back.

"Does this gun back here work?" yelled Ilana.

"Yeah, just be careful not to shoot off the tail of the plane."

On the ground Emídio heard the plane approaching again. Looking up at it from the remains of a barracks where he had taken cover, he saw it heading straight for...

"NOOOOOOOO!!!!"

Simultaneously the machine guns of the Hawker Hart Demon and Max's M16 spit lead, and liquid began to pour in streams from the large, elevated tank in front of them marked *combustível* - fuel.

"Not enough!" yelled Max. "Ilana, give it all you got with your gun as we pass."

The plane banked and Ilana took careful aim. Her fingers pressed hard on the trigger and a steady stream of bullets flew straight into the tank.

On the ground Emídio watched helplessly as it burst into a wall of flame. The little biplane was buffeted in the air by the force of the explosion. Ray had to pull hard on the stick to maintain control.

"Home James!" Max shouted above him, and Ray leaned the plane towards Santo Expedito.

On the ground, Doctor Emídio Santana was beside himself with rage. "A phone!!!!" he screamed. "Somebody bring me a *maldito* telephone!!!"

But that was not an easy task. All the phone lines had been effectively destroyed by the surprise attack.

"Thirty years!!!" he screamed again, at nobody in particular. "My master plan of thirty years, in RUINS!!! And all because of a *missionary!!!*" The last word was not spoken, it was spat.

"Sir?" It was the commander. "We found a satellite phone."

Emídio grabbed the phone and began punching the numbers furiously. His hair - normally coifed to perfection - was disheveled. His eyes were wild and his teeth bared in uncontrollable anger. He held the phone to his ear.

"Hello! Ferraz!" There was no attempt at formality. "This is Emídio Santana. The *americano* got away. Right now he is in a biplane..." There was a pause. "That's what I said. A BIPLANE! Stop your idiot questions and listen. The plane is headed toward Santo Expedito. You need to scramble two army helicopters immediately and shoot them down...no...wait. Don't shoot them down. Force them to land at the airport and have the whole army there to meet them. DO NOT LET THEM ESCAPE!"

Emídio took a breath. In a calmer voice he continued. "Also, send a helicopter to the Ipuna river valley to pick me up and take me to the airport. I want to deal with them myself." Another pause. "IT MAKES NO DIFFERENCE WHAT I AM DOING HERE! JUST SEND A CHOPPER TO PICK ME UP!!!"

Santana pressed the *disconnect* button forcefully, and was about to hand the phone back to the base commander when he thought better. Once again he punched in a number and held the phone to his ears.

"Hello Diego? We have a situation..."

Francesca was finding it hard to hide her elation. Inácio and Itamar had extracted enough information from a very frightened Cascavel to indicate that perhaps Max had made it through the night. Why else would the American taxi driver fly off in that direction first thing this morning. She had often wondered about the old man's loyalties. Now she was certain that he was intent on helping his compatriot.

The three military helicopters screaming over the mansion minutes earlier were another good sign. She knew they were headed in the direction of the jungle, where her husband (she shuddered at the word) Emídio had gone that morning. Standing on the veranda that commanded a splendid view of Santo Expedito, she looked through her binoculars. Her keen eyes saw a convoy of military vehicles making its way through the downtown traffic.

"Towards the airport," she muttered.

Contrary to the dominant opinion, most supermodels are indeed highly intelligent. It takes a keen mind and intense business acumen to make it big in the competitive fashion industry. And

Francesca Almeida da Silva Santana had made it to the top of that game as a young girl. Thus it required no special effort on her part to figure out what was going on.

Francesca put down the binoculars picked up the phone. "*Senhor* Rockwell, I have good news, and bad news."

"We've got company...nine o'clock."

At Max's warning Ray swiveled his head to the left. Flying parallel to him was an attack helicopter bearing the markings of the Cabrito army.

"...and at three o'clock."

Another one, to the right. There was no chance of escape. The little biplane - ruler of the skies over a peaceful Great Britain of the 1930s - would be no match in speed for the modern choppers. Their twin Gatling guns could chew up the lightly armored aircraft in a matter of seconds.

Ilana had seen them too and swiveled around to look at the men, concern on her face.

"If they wanted to shoot us, they would have done so by now. This is an official escort," Ray surmised.

"Right," agreed Max. "Question is, where are we being escorted to."

Ray shrugged. "If I had to guess, I'd say the airport."

CHAPTER 21

A LITTLE MORE CONVERSATION

James Rockwell was in his room. He had been awaiting Francesca's call. As soon as his newly arrived guest finished freshening up they would have to leave, and quickly. He phoned the front desk and asked them to have his personal limo -the one provided to him by the government - ready as quickly as possible.

There was a knock on the door. Looking out the peephole, Rockwell saw the smiling face of Conchita, the prettily little masseuse. He opened the door.

"I'm sorry, there's not going to be time for a massa...." he stopped in mid sentence as he found himself staring into the barrel of a pistol. Looking at Conchita he found she was no longer smiling.

"You will call and cancel your request for the limo," she said in a hard voice that brooked no argument. She indicated the phone with a movement of her chin.

Slowly, cautiously, never taking his eyes off the gun, James Rockwell began to back up toward the phone. "Are you sure this is a good idea?" he asked. "After all, I am here at the direct request of Dr. Santana."

Chonchita's lips curled in a mirthless smile. "So am I," she replied.

"I see. Well, in that case, I am very sorry."

"Sorry for what?" asked the masseuse/enforcer.

"Sorry for the headache you are going to have when you wake up."

There was only time for Conchita's brow to furrow in confusion before she sunk to the ground, unconscious. Behind her, holding a now-broken bottle, stood Rockwell's guest.

"Should we tie her up?" she asked.

"No time. We need to get to the airport, yesterday!"

The bandido known as Cascavel was staggering through Santo Expedito, where he had been wandering aimlessly since his "conversation" with the two burly Brazilians. He knew it would be no use for him to return to Diego after failing him twice. He had no idea what to do, or where to go. *Failure. Weak. Incompetent. Bandit. Bad man!* The accusations screamed in his brain. Looking up, he noticed he was standing next to the Paladar Dourado. Right below the terrace where he had failed so singularly a few weeks ago.

It would have been better if I had fallen to the pavement instead of in the trash can. It would have put me out of my misery.

Despair gripped him and put a terrible idea in his head. He went to the wall and began to climb.

Something had gone horribly wrong; that much was plain to Diego. He was not privy to Santana's grand project, but from the phone call he had just received it was obvious that things were not well with his boss. One thing he knew: the americano and the girl were still alive, and so was Raimundo. He would have to deal with Cascavel later. Right now, he was under orders to not let Max leave the island...alive.

He leaned forward in the seat of the military transport as it sped through the streets of Santo Expedito. "Faster!" he urged the driver. They were at the head of a column of military vehicles headed at breakneck speed toward the airport. Sirens were screaming. Midday traffic was trying desperately, and somewhat unsuccessfully, to get out of the way of the army caravan.

"There!" he shouted, seeing an opportunity. "Turn right at the next block!"

There was barely time to make the maneuver, but somehow the driver managed and they barreled down the vacant road. The rest of the caravan followed. Diego fingered his rifle in eager anticipation.

Cascavel stood on one of the wooden beams that protruded from the top floor of the building that housed the Paladar Doutrado restaurant. It was the same beam from which he had tried, unsuccessfully, to spy on the americano and his lady friend a few weeks earlier. Now he stood on it, perfectly balanced.

My life is worth nothing, he thought. *I am a failure, a coward, a bandido.* He looked down for a moment, and almost lost his nerve. But then he closed his eyes, took a deep breath, spread out his arms, and executed a perfect swan dive.

Bernardinho stood in the doorway of his house and stroked his chin. He had just been to Missionary Max's home, and nobody was there. His conversation with Ray and the police officers the previous morning was still on his mind. Then there were the helicopters that had gone screaming overhead in the direction of the jungle. Now his ears picked up the sirens wailing in the center of the capital. An uneasiness gripped him. He remembered the plans he had been making with the Blakes before they left - plans to reach the Yamani Indians with the gospel. Then, without warning, the Blake's had gone.

Now Max had gone to the jungle and not returned. Somehow the Cabritan man knew that all the commotion he was hearing had something to do with his American friend, the new leader of their small congregation. Quickly Bernardinho opened the door and went inside. "Isabela!" he called.

"Yes father?"

"I want you and your mother to call everybody in the congregation. Tell them to meet here at our house for a prayer meeting."

"A prayer meeting?"

"Yes. I think Missionary Max is in trouble."

Death had been a lot easier than Cascavel expected. Instead of the hard, unforgiving cobblestone pavement, the landing had been soft, almost...cushiony. Now a pleasant, wind-like sensation blew over him and there was a rushing noise, not unlike a...a... truck engine?

Cascavel opened his eyes, and slowly comprehension dawned on him. He had not landed on the pavement after all, but on the canvas covering of a troop transport as it passed the Paladar Dourado.

I am such a failure I can't even commit suicide successfully, he mused bitterly, even as he grabbed hold of the edges of the canvas and held on for dear life.

Raising his head, he looked around. He was on the last vehicle in a long convoy.

I wonder where we are going? Almost immediately his question was answered as the truck turned, slowed down, and came to a stop.

The airport!

Soldiers boiled out of the back of the transports and lined the runway. Tanks and armored vehicles placed themselves at either end. Cascavel ducked down to avoid being seen, but there was not much danger of that; all attention was focused on the sky. Cascavel followed their gaze.

Two helicopters were approaching, and between them, a bi-plane.

Max looked down at runway before them, lined with tanks and soldiers.

He had briefly entertained the idea of making a run for it as soon as they touched down. Clearly, that was not an option.

"Looks like there's a party going on, and our attendance is mandatory." Ray grumbled.

"If we make any evasive maneuvers they will rip us to shreds," Max said. "I think we are going to have to play along for now."

"Even if there was any chance of getting away, where would we go? There's not enough gas to get us to any of the outlying islands."

"Why do you think they are so upset?" Max asked.

"I'm thinking it might have something to do with the fact that we just destroyed their little drug operation." Ray replied with a chuckle. And then, "Well, no sense delaying the fireworks." With that he pushed the stick forward and nosed the plane down towards the runway.

As the plane taxied down the runway Max analyzed their situation. It dawned on him that this was the third time in twenty-four hours that he had been surrounded by a hostile enemy. These guys brought a lot more firepower, he noted.

The plane came to a stop and the engine cut out. Immediately soldiers approached the plane, weapons leveled at its occupants. A voice came over a loud speaker.

"Get out of the plane with your hands raised!"

With no other options, all three complied. Max jumped down from his perch and helped Ilana to the ground. Finally Ray climbed from the cockpit and all three stood by the plane, hands in the air.

For several minutes nothing happened. The opposing parties stood looking at each other. Not a word was spoken. Max was beginning to wonder if they would spend all day like that, when the sound of another helicopter reached his ears. Glancing up he saw a military aircraft identical to the ones that had escorted them to the runway. It landed on the tarmac, dust blowing around it and before the blades stopped their swirling the door opened and out jumped Emídio Santana.

Max was shocked at how the man had transformed. Once impeccably groomed, Santana was now wild-eyed and disheveled, his dark suit torn and smudged. Max even thought he caught a whiff of smoke as the man approached them.

Suddenly, Santana drew a pistol from his coat pocket and pointed it shakily at Max and his companions.

"You!" he said. "You...meddling American missionary! You infernal busybody! You could not leave well enough alone! How dare you interfere in my plans?"

Max suppressed the anger that was welling up within him. The deranged millionaire was speaking in English. Max switched to Portuguese, speaking loud enough for everybody to hear.

"You mean that drug operation we just destroyed was yours?" Max asked feigning innocence. "I had no idea that Cabrito's leading citizen would be involved in such a sordid affair."

"Shut up! You have no idea what you are talking about!" Max could see that Santana's knuckles were white as he gripped the pistol. The weapon trembled in his hand.

"You are a traitor to the people of this island, and especially to the Yamani's!" It was Ilana, and she was livid. Max looked at her, stunned. Her beautiful eyes bored accusingly into Santana. "You told me you wanted to protect them. You liar! You were just using them as a shield for your drug operation. You should be ashamed!"

"Ilana, Ilana." Santana addressed the girl in a creepily condescending tone. "You could have had everything. A high government position, prestige, honor...and me!"

Ilana spat. "I want no part of you, Emídio Santana. You are just an office boy for your father, a spoiled brat who thinks he gets everything he wants. Well, I have news for you, you...you..." Words failed her.

"Overblown two-bit wannabe?" Max suggested.

"Yes...what he said!" Ilana completed.

Santana shook his head sadly. "Ilana, you probably know that you are going to die here on this tarmac. What you don't know is that you are going to die in front of your father."

"Wha..." Ilana was taken aback. Max looked at her, and then at Ray. The old soldier's face was beet red with rage.

"Why you..." he started forward and immediately Max's hand shot out to restrain him. uddenly it all became quite clear to the younger American.

"You see," he continued, "years ago a simple American man named Raymond Sand came to see me. He was in...how do the Americans put it...a cucumber."

"It's 'pickle,'" corrected Max.

"SHUT UP!" Santana shouted at him, waiving his gun. Then, in a calmer voice. "This American, this Raymond Sand, had fornicated with a Yamani woman, and Raymond was concerned about the well-being of the little girl who was born as a result. Being the generous man that I am, I offered to help, guaranteeing an education to that little girl, in exchange of the services of Mr. Raymond."

"Please no..." Ray protested. It was no use.

"These services," Santana continued, warming up to his tale, "these services included helping me remove several foreigners who were causing me problems, interfering with my plans. Specifically, the missionaries."

Max looked at Ray surprised. Ray hung his head.

"Raymond was successful at removing all of them. All but one. And I am going to take care of that one right now."

"Ray?" Max looked at the old man.

"It's all true," the old man said, tears of shame streaming down his face. "I only wanted to protect my daughter. I am a bad, bad man."

Ilana stepped over and took the old man's head in her hands, lifting his face to hers. "Ray...Father!"

"Oh, Ilana!" Ray sobbed. "My whole life I wanted to hear you call me that. I just wish..."

Santana let out a maniacal laugh. "You just wish it wasn't as your beloved daughter was about to die." The disheveled, wild-eyed millionaire brought his pistol to bear on Ilana. Max moved to step in front of her, but she put her hand on his shoulder. "It's okay," she said.

Max looked at her, quizzically.

"There in the jungle," she whispered, "I believed. I'm not afraid." She stepped out in front of Max and faced Santana without flinching. "Did you hear that, *senhor* Santana? I am not afraid of you."

As if in slow motion Max watched as the madman's finger began to tighten around the trigger.

CHAPTER 22

RUNWAY RUCKUS

Bernardinho surveyed the group of people gathered at his home. "Brothers, I called you here because I believe that our friend Missionary Max is in deep trouble." Briefly he related the things he had observed and the conclusions he had drawn.

"It's true." It was João Carlos, who had abandoned his *bodega* in the city center and ridden his motorcycle full tilt to the emergency meeting. "I watched a convoy of military vehicles pass through the city. They went right in front of my store."

The other members nodded, and several others related similar observations.

"If this does indeed have something to do with our friend, he is in grave danger." Bernardinho observed.

"So what can we do?" It was his wife.

"Only one thing we can do: pray." Without another word the members of the small congregation bowed their heads, and the sound of simple, heartfelt intercession filled the room.

"You are very courageous, Ilana." Emídio Santana was squinting down the bore of his pistol at the beautiful girl in front of him. "Pity you are about to die. You and I would have been great together."

Ilana spat. "I would die before that happened!"

"How prophetic."

The sound of a blaring horn and squealing tires caused Santana to blink and turn around. Max breathed a sigh of relief. The soldiers standing around them swung their guns around to meet the newcomer - who was arriving in style. The long, black limo sped down the runway, apparently heedless of the soldiers in its path. The hood was decorated with two flags that were flapping furiously in the wind: that of the United States and on the right, and that of Sherman Pharmaceutical Group, International on the left.

The soldiers, caught completely by surprise, parted, and the limo passed through them without slowing and came to a screeching halt beside Santana, almost knocking him over. The back door opened and out jumped James Madison Rockwell.

"What is the meaning of this?" he demanded.

"I see no reason for you to be involved in this, Mr. Rockwell," said Santana icily. "This is an internal affair of the Cabritan government, and it would be wise for you not to interfere."

"On the contrary," replied the businessman, and Santana was shocked to realize that he was being addressed in perfect Portuguese. "This has everything to do with the Sherman Pharmaceutical Group, International."

"How?" demanded Santana.

Rockwell's voice was smooth as oil. "First, it has come to my attention that there was a plan afoot to use the presence of our company on this island as a pretext for the shipping of illicit drugs to the US. As you can imagine, the board is very concerned about this, and has asked me to meet with you immediately. Why don't you come back to the hotel with me and we can get to the bottom of this together? I'm sure something can be worked out."

Max suddenly had a whole new respect for Mr. Rockwell.

"No!" Santana was livid. "These people have committed high crimes against my...against the government and they will pay the price!" He swung his pistol back toward the three standing by the plane.

"*Senhor* Santana," Rockwell's voice never changed it's tone, "I don't think that would be a very good idea."

"And why not, *senhor* Rockwell?" sneered Santana. "I am in charge here. What I say goes. And I say that these three must die!"

"Don't say I didn't warn you," said Rockwell, and shrugged. Turning, he nodded to the chauffeur who opened the back door of the limousine. Out stepped the most formidable woman Santana had ever seen. Her gray hair, streaked with black, was pulled back severely into a bun. Her slim frame was dressed in a black power suit with grey pinstripes. Black gloves were on her hands, and black high-heels on her feet. Her back was ramrod straight and her jaw was set. The expression on her face said "don't mess with me."

Her grey eyes scanned the scene, taking in everything. Then they fixed on Max. She walked directly to him completely ignoring the puzzled Santana and his gun. Standing not two feet in front of him, she looked him in the eye.

"Hello, Maxwell."

Max shook his head in wonder and a wry smile spread across his face. "Hi, Mom."

From his perch on top of the truck Cascavel watched the whole scene. Forgotten was the fact that moments ago he had tried to commit suicide. Now he was totally involved in the drama playing out before him.

Cowards! He thought to himself. *They are all cowards. All of these soldiers and guns for three people. And the biggest coward of all is senhor Santana.*

Out of the corner of his eye, Cascavel saw Diego crouching beside truck. Pressed against his shoulder was the stock of a high-powered rifle, and he was carefully adjusting the sights. Cascaval could not know about the conversation between O Diabo and Santana earlier, where the would-be drug kingpin had told his lackey to make sure that the three fugitives did not leave the tarmac alive. The erstwhile bandido had not been privy to that conversation, but it did not take a genius to see what were the intentions of his "benefactor" were.

No, he is the biggest coward of all, Cascavel reflected. *There he is, hidden from view, where nobody can see him or stop him. Nobody except...*

Slowly, he inched his way forward.

Ilana was in a daze. In the space of the last two hours she had narrowly escaped death three times, found a new faith, learned that the old taxi driver/pilot was her father, and now, that her friend Max was the son of the CEO of Sherman Pharmaceutical Group, International.

Regina Sherman was speaking to her son.

"The last time we talked you were working a construction job near Albany. Now I find you breaking up a drug ring on Cabrito. You really should write more."

Max looked sheepish. "I'm sorry Mom. You haven't been exactly happy with my choices lately."

"You're right, I haven't. But I must admit, I am very curious about how you came to find out about this drug plot, and what motivated you to take such drastic action. You could have just called, you know. Whatever the case, it is a rather dramatic way to return to the fold."

"Mom, I'm not..."

But she was not looking at him. She was looking at Ilana. The younger woman was somewhat uncomfortable under her gaze.

"Care to introduce me to your new girlfriend?"

"Mom! She's not..."

Santana, forgotten but still holding his pistol, interrupted. The presence of the CEO had forced him to regain some of his dignified manner, but he could no longer stand to be ignored.

"Madam, I must protest. These people have committed high crimes against the people of Cabrito and they are currently in our custody."

Regina Sherman turned to him with a look of absolute scorn. "They have done no such thing, and you will do well to take your thugs and go back to doing whatever it is you do all day when you are not running a drug operation or threatening the lives of innocent people."

Ray snorted. "Doesn't leave him with many options."

Santana was speechless. To be addressed that way...and by a woman!!!

"I have the power here!" he shouted. "I am Emídio Santana! I am in charge! I will have you all thrown in jail!"

"No, I don't think you will." Regina said. For Ilana it was easy to see where Max got his icy coolness under fire. Like mother like son.

"I will not take orders from you!"

"As you wish." she replied simply, then turned to Mr. Rockwell, who was leaning casually on the hood of the limousine. "James, did you make the phone call I asked you to?"

"But of course," he replied. Reaching into his inside coat pocket he produced his satellite phone, which he handed to Santana. "It's for you."

Not knowing what to think, Santana put the phone to his ear.

"*Alô?*"

At once his face went completely white. His eyes widened, and his mouth moved, but no sound came out. Finally he spoke, "But father...."

More silence. As Santana listened to the person on the other end his expression changed from surprise to rage to frustration and back to rage. Finally, there was submission.

"Yes father. As you wish." He hung up and scowled at the people in front of him. Regina Sherman gave him a sweet smile.

"So tell me, how is my old friend George Santana?"

Santana did not answer. He was trembling with rage, struggling to bring himself under control. Finally he turned to Max, Ilana, and Ray.

"You are free to go," he said, between clenched teeth. Then he turned stiffly on his heels and walked to his own limo.

Back by the transport vehicle Diego was watching all the proceedings with detached interest. He was too far away to hear the conversations, but obviously things were not going well for Santana. It made no difference, Diego was his insurance that the three would indeed be dead shortly.

The soldiers had lowered their guns, and were waiting for instructions. Santana was heading toward his limo, and the three targets, along with the newcomer, were moving in the direction of the large SPGI helicopter. Diego waited for the signal.

There it was! Santana looked in his direction and nodded. Diego looked down his sights. A clean shot. First the missionário, then the girl, then the old man. It would be so easy. He took a deep breath and then...

"*COVARDE!!!!!*"

The word, which was half a shout, half an accusation, came from above him. Diego looked up just as Cascavel came crashing down on top of him. The rifle clattered to the ground. Diego clawed for it, but Cascavel was faster. He leapt on it and wheeled around, pointing it at the still-sprawled Diego.

"*Levanta, seu covarde!* Get up, you coward!"

Over by the helicopters everybody's attention turned to the two men. Cascavel was pointing the rifle at Diego's head.

"I said get up!"

Slowly Diego obeyed.

"Hands in the air!" ordered Cascavel. Once again the other man complied, his eyes darting toward Santana - who was the only one pretending not to notice - and back to the rifle which was now right before his face.

"You are a coward," Cascavel spat at him. "A filthy coward. You try to hurt these innocent people, because you are a pathetic coward. Say it! Say you are a coward."

The jabbing gun in his face left Diego no choice. "I am a coward," he mumbled.

"Louder! So everybody can hear."

"I am a coward."

"Who burnt down the church? Tell them!"

"I did it."

"Who ordered you to burn it down?"

"Santana did."

"And why did you obey him?"

Diego drew a blank.

"It's because you are a coward. Say it! Say you obeyed Santana because you are a coward."

"I obeyed Santana because I am a coward."

"Yes you are, and now you are going to die like a coward!"

The old Max Sherman, the Green Beret Max Sherman, would have probably watched Diego die with some satisfaction, seeing his demise as the simple removal of a potential threat. The new Max Sherman, however, could not bear the thought of what would surely happen to Diego after he left his mortal body. With this in mind, and oblivious to the protests of his companions, he sprinted past the stunned soldiers towards the two antagonists.

"Cascavel! Wait! Don't shoot!"

Cascavel kept his gaze firmly on his intended victim. "This man is a coward. He deserves to die."

Max came up beside him. He made no attempt to reach for the gun. "You're right, he does."

Diego's knees gave out and he sank, trembling, to the ground. Max continued. "But then again, so do all of us. I was merciful to you twice, and God has been merciful to both you and me. So we should show mercy to this man."

"Please, mercy!" begged the thoroughly frightened Diego. Slowly, Cascavel lowered the gun. "I do not understand why you would do this" he said, "but you are a man of courage, and I will listen to what you have to say."

Max put his hand on Cascavel's shoulder. "You are a brave man, Cascavel. It is an honor to call you friend." Then he turned to Diego. "I think you had better leave...fast."

Diego needed no convincing. He scrambled to his feet and disappeared.

"Come with us, Cascavel. Is that your real name?"

Cascavel grinned. "No, my mother was a big fan of a great American president. She named me after him: Nixon."

"Why don't we stick with Cascavel," said Max quickly. "Right now I need to have a heart-to-heart with Dr. Santana."

Just then the door of Santana's helicopter slammed and the blades churned to life. Max, Ilana, Ray, Cascavel, Regina, James, and the cadre of soldiers watched as Santana's chopper rose into the air and disappeared quickly in the direction from whence it had come.

Having no orders, and nobody to give them, the soldiers dispersed to their transports and one by one they drove off.

"Well, I think my work is done here." It was Regina Sherman. Through the whole ordeal she had never lost her poise. She straightened her power jacket, and then turned to her son. "Maxwell, when you get back to New York we will talk about your position with our company."

"Mom...I...I'm not going back to New York."

She looked at him, then over at Ilana. "Oh, I see. You can bring her too."

"No, Mom, that's not it." *Here it comes*, he thought, and took a deep breath. "You see, Mom, I'm...I'm a missionary."

For the first time that day Regina Sherman was taken by surprise. "You! A missionary? When did you get religion'"

"I didn't 'get religion,' Mom. I met Jesus."

Mrs. Sherman snorted. "Seriously, Max, you will have to come up with a better excuse than that. It's okay, you can tell me you are in love with the girl. I understand."

Max sighed. "Mom, I came here to help some missionaries with a construction project. Santana intimidated them and they left just as I was arriving. I decided to stay. The church here needs me, and there is a lot to be done here. It's...it's what God wants me to do."

There was a short silence. Finally Regina spoke. "So my little boy is a missionary. Well, your grandmother would be happy, anyway." She turned to the girl. "We still have not been properly introduced."

"Oh, I'm sorry," Max apologized. "Mom, this is Ilana. Ilana, my Mother."

"A pleasure." said Ilana, still somewhat dazed.

"The pleasure is all mine. Max, religion or no, take care of her. And James," she turned Mr. Rockwell, "keep an eye out for my boy. George Santana and I go way back, and our company has... shall we say...leverage on him, so he is not going to try anything overt. But he is a tricky old coot, and he most certainly knew and approved of his son's foray into 'pharmaceuticals'. Now I'm going to go home. This heat is starting to make my mascara run."

EPILOGUE

The alarm went off in Max's ear, and slowly, reluctantly he got up. Shaking the sleepiness from his head he shuffled to the bathroom where he brushed his teeth, washed his face, and brought his shock of red hair under a semblance of control. Then he went into the hallway and down the stairs, intent on some breakfast. Halfway down the stairs, he sniffed.

Coffee? But who...

"Good morning, Max." The voice belonged to Mr. Rockwell.

Max shook his head and continued on down the stairs.

"You know James, you could just call."

"I know, but I find surprise visits much more effective. I hope you don't mind, I took the liberty of putting coffee on. You don't drink decaf, do you?"

"Nope, straight up." Max flopped onto the couch in front of the chair where the SPGI representative was sitting. "To what do I owe the pleasure of your visit this time?"

"Oh nothing in particular. Just checking up on you. Your mother was very specific as per her instructions to me."

"Great. So now I have a babysitter."

"Max, Max. Is that any way to thank the guy who got you out of a - shall we say - sticky situation?"

"I already did thank Him...or perhaps you weren't referring to God."

James Rockwell chuckled. "I'm not a religious man myself, but it is obvious Somebody besides your mother was looking out for you that day. So how are your friends?"

"I imagine you know about Ilana," Max replied.

"Oh indeed. She is doing a marvelous job as our secretary for indigenous relations. A big help in negotiating for the raw materials we need. Although I suspect she sometimes gives them more favorable terms than is absolutely necessary. Still, nice to have someone on board who understands the tribespeople."

"Right," Max replied. "She has also been pretty busy cleaning up her Dad's place."

"You mean Ray's run-down old farm?"

"Exactly. Just that it's not quite so run down anymore. Ilana's feminine touch has done wonders for the place."

"And the church?" asked Mr. Rockwell. "How is that little project going?"

"Better than I had hoped. I have absolutely no experience in leading a church, but God seems to be making up the difference. We have had a few converts, and every Sunday we have visitors. Interestingly, after that little episode on the tarmac, several of the soldiers brought their families. It would seem that Santana's stock with the military took a dive that day."

James chuckled. "I wonder why? Still, don't underestimate the guy. He and his Dad are up to no good. They are not the kind to let bygones be bygones."

"Thanks for the heads-up," Max replied.

After some more inconsequential chatter Max accompanied James Rockwell to the door. Despite the older man's unorthodox way of making his presence known, the visit had been pleasant. Now Max's attention turned to the activities of the day: a morning

jog, an afternoon Bible study with Ilana and Ray, and final preparations for tomorrow's message.

As he was about to close the door, he noticed that there was a
letter in the mailbox attached to the wall. He picked it up and read
the return address: Mary Sue Perkins.

Oh, right...my girlfriend!

Quickly he tore open the envelope. The letter inside was per-
fumed and decorated with stickers portraying hearts and teddy
bears:

Dear Max,

*You have been gone for so long. I can only imagine how much you
must miss me. Thank you for the nice earrings you sent.*

*Pastor Dave tells me that you are a missionary now. I figured
that, since you only accepted Christ four years ago, you must be really struggling. You probably need somebody with a lot more experience in the faith to help you.*

*That is why I have decided to come visit you next month. Please
make sure to arrange a comfortable place to stay. I am very excited
to be able to talk to you and make plans for our future together. I
also hope to be able to minister to the poor natives of Cabrito.*

Love,

Your Mary Sue

As he folded the letter and put it back into the envelope Max
realized that his heart beat faster at the thought of Mary Sue's visit.

The problem was that he couldn't tell if it was beating with anticipation or dread. Then his mind turned involuntarily to Ilana.

It's dread, he finally admitted to himself. *Definitely dread.*

The End

ABOUT THE AUTHOR

Andrew Comings is a Baptist missionary working in the state of Maranhão, Brazil. He is married to Itacyara, and they have two children, Michael and Nathanael. Their ministry includes church planting, theological training, and camp ministry. In his spare time Andrew writes, plays the saxophone, and dreams about having Brazil's largest model train set. You can learn more about their work - including the latest from the world of Missionary Max - at their website: andrewcomings.com

ABOUT THE ILLUSTRATOR

Zilson Costa is an artist and author from the Brazilian state of Maranhão. He graduated in fine arts from the Federal University of Maranhão and serves as a musician and art professor in local schools. His artwork has been featured in some of the premier comic book publishers of Brazil, and he has collaborated with well-known artists from Brazil and from the US.

Made in the USA
Charleston, SC
13 April 2016